Capricious

Issue Nine ❧ January 2018

First published in New Zealand in 2018 by Capricious Publications.

www.capricioussf.org

Contents

Editorial

Welcome to this ninth issue of Capricious, and our first special issue, a collection of speculative fiction that includes gender diverse pronouns – pronouns including singular they, neopronouns, and pronoun sets of the authors' invention. I am delighted – and honoured – to bring you this collection of stories by Nino Cipri, Bogi Takács, Lauren E. Mitchell, A.E. Prevost, Cameron Van Sant, Rem Wigmore, Penny Stirling, Hazel Gold, SL Byrne, and Rae White.

These are stories of exploration and love, of travelling far away and of coming home. They are stories of dragons and aliens, spaceships and humans. Of the weight of history and of new beginnings. I hope you as a reader will find something in these pages that excites you, something that resonates with your experience, or something that introduces you to new ideas or new perspectives.

What are gender diverse pronouns and why did I decide to collect these stories? I answered the 'what' in the crowdfunding campaign for this issue thus:

A pronoun – or, more specifically in this case, a personal pronoun – is a word you can use in place of someone's name. Rather than saying "Ryan picked up the book but Ryan decided it wasn't the sort of thing Ryan enjoyed reading" you would more typically say "Ryan picked up the book but she decided it wasn't the sort of thing she enjoyed reading". She is the personal pronoun.

In English, the personal pronouns we're most used to are he and she. Not only do these require the speaker to know the gender of the person they're talking about, but they only properly cover two genders. Humans don't always fit in these boxes.

Fortunately, there are a range of gender neutral pronouns – and they're not all modern inventions. They are used mainly to either refer to an individual for whom "he" or "she" isn't appropriate (that individual might identify as non-binary or genderqueer) or for a hypothetical person whose gender is not established ("when you find out who the person in charge is, tell them I need to talk to them").

What's the difference between gender neutral and gender diverse pronouns? There's significant overlap between the two, but I chose the "gender diverse" terminology for this project because we also welcome stories in which pronouns do signify a specific gender, but in different ways to he and she.

In these stories, the pronouns include ze/zir, ze/hir, ey/eir/em, pry/preer/prin, e/eir/em and more, as well as singular they. Some stories - like Rae White's "Glitter and Leaf Litter", and Cameron Van Sant's "Phaser", show characters making individual journeys to find the appropriate pronouns for them, in environments where only "he" and "she" are considered the norm. Others create different worlds with their own language and conceptions of gender; A.E. Prevost's "Sandals Full of Rainwater" follows a migrant from one fictional country, building a new life in another, whose language learning – and sense of identity – is impacted by the new concept of gendered pronouns.

As to the 'why', I wanted most of all to help some more stories like this into the world. So much of the conversation around gender diverse pronouns is reactive, a – necessary and understandable – self justification. It's of people forced to explain themselves, forced to justify their existence. It's frustration at being misgendered again and again and having your right to exist subject to – usually not very knowledgeable – grammatical arguments. That's an annoying consequence of the world we live in, and is fairly represented in some of these stories. But it's not all there is. If you can get past that, there's magic and creativity. There are really bad twitter puns. There are pretty enamel pronoun pins. There are thoughts about this world, and worlds to come, about language and languages and how they compare and fit together.

More than anything, I wanted to provide a space for some of that creativity. To be a space where authors don't have to worry that their work will be dismissed because "singular they is bad grammar" or "these new words are confusing" but to be free to experiment. To talk about their own experiences (while this project was open to authors of all genders, a significant number of those who submitted – and those whose work is included in these pages – identified themselves as non-binary) and to imagine different worlds.

A complaint that often occurs is that people aren't used to pronoun sets other than he/him/his and she/her and it's hard to learn them. Sometimes that complaint is disingenuous (often accompanied by stories of highly dubious veracity), but sometimes it reflects a genuine uncertainty or difficulty. To which my response is, how can we make it easier for those who genuinely want to do better to do so? And the answer is to normalise them. To use them in conversation, yes, but also in our stories, in fiction in all media. In stories about spaceships and about magic, heroism and exploration, families and home.

This volume is a drop in the ocean in that regard, but I know it's not alone.

So the ten stories in these pages are connected by their use of gender diverse pronouns, either singular they, or what are often termed neopronouns, a recently constructed pronoun set for the express purpose of not signifying a binary gender. In some cases, the pronoun sets the authors chose are in existing usage, in others the author made them up for the purpose of their story. Sometimes these pronouns are used primarily to signify a non-binary character or characters, sometimes they are used to portray worlds that conceive gender differently to the society the author is from, sometimes they are part of a more general exploration of gender.

In all other regards, these stories are very different. They are stories of love in all the forms it takes, and of heartbreak. Stories of travel, by road and by spaceship. Stories of family tensions and new families found. Stories of revenge and of reconciliation. Stories set from Kansas to Australia and out into the far flung reaches of space.

They are wide-ranging, but this is far from a comprehensive collection; there are many stories that came before this issue and there are gaps that I would have liked to fill better. Towards the end of this volume

I have included a list of some other science fiction and fantasy stories which use gender diverse pronouns; I hope it will be a starting point for those who would like to read further.

I am indebted to many people in the creation of this issue, in particular to those who showed faith in this project right from the start by supporting the crowdfunding campaign which made it possible, and whose names are listed at the end of this volume. Thank you to the authors for their patience, diligence, and most of all their wonderful words, to everyone else who submitted stories, many of which were very high quality, and to Laya Rose who created cover art so good I keep staring at it and wanting to tell people how much I love details like the rain in the window and the glow around the succulents. Thank you to my partner, Kelly, who is responsible for much of the design of Capricious, including the hedgehog section breaks, as well as making sure I didn't *die* midway through editing due to forgetting to drink water (I forget to drink water a lot).

And lastly, thank you to all of you who offered words of encouragement or support, who shared our crowdfunding campaign or our call for submissions, and who wrote or shared stories that, long before this issue was even conceived of, helped me believe there was a space for people of all genders in the worlds we imagine as well as the world we live in.

– A.C. Buchanan, January 2018

Ad Astra Per Aspera

Nino Cipri

I'm pretty sure I lost my gender in Kansas.

(This space is reserved for any *Wizard of Oz* reference you might make. I'm not sure how you could relate it to gender, but whenever I mention Kansas, it's the first thing people want to do. So go ahead, if you're into that.)

Anyway, it's true. I was driving west across the pancaked landscape, the flat and yearning winter fields, and I realized I hadn't seen my gender in a while. Not since Wichita at least, and that had been several hours and many radio stations before: Christian talk shows, country songs, odd interruptions of metal or hardcore music.

I lose things all the time, especially when traveling. On my first big roadtrip across the country, I drove away from Philadelphia while my bag was still on the trunk of the car. Goodbye to my journal—no great loss there; goodbye to my digital camera and cell phone, because this was back in the days when those were separate items; goodbye to my book of Arthur Rimbaud's poetry that I had found in a used bookstore in Colorado two weeks earlier. Oh, and goodbye to my

15

wallet—someone found it and spent $180 at PetSmart before I canceled it.

I wonder if some Kansan will pick up my gender the way that someone picked up my bag, twelve years ago in Philadelphia. Will they pick through my gender's many pockets? Discard that dollar-bin paperback of *The Drunken Boat*, but keep my great-aunt Ethel's wedding ring, which was so small I only could wear it on my pinky? Toss the electric-blue lipstick that I could never make myself wear, but rub the cedar cologne onto the soft creases of their wrist and neck?

Is there a lost-and-found forum for genders? Maybe I should make a sign and staple it to every billboard in every truckstop along I-70, the way you might for a dog that took off or a cat that slunk through a barely-open window. "LOST: One gender, not particularly adherent to notions of sexual dimorphism. Answers to Spivak pronouns or they/them. Hostile when cornered."

(This is a placeholder for your judgment, even your disgust. What kind of irresponsible twit loses their gender? If *you* had a gender as nice as mine, you would have taken better care of it. Maybe you're thinking that this might be some sort of *millennial* thing. All these millennials with their *boutique* and *artisanal* genders, and this is what they do with them?)

To be honest, this isn't even the first time I've lost track of my gender. My mother constantly had to remind me to take it with me when I was still in high school. "Got your books? Got your keys? Got your gender?" I was always losing my gender in my debris-filled bedroom. And if it came down to either getting to work or school on time, or finding my gender, what was I supposed to do?

The first time I went outside without my gender, I expected to stop traffic, to be publicly denounced at the bus stop and library, everywhere that decent, gender-respecting people lived. In the end, I got a few unfriendly stares, but a couple people told me that I was really brave for not needing my gender all the time. They were the people that wheeled their genders around like oxygen tanks or carried them in slings like babies.

(This space might be a place for you to pause, and wonder how you carry your own gender, how close or how distant you might hold it to your skin.)

Something tells me that this time around, my gender might be gone for good; that it's somewhere in the acres of horizon behind me. Maybe—and I know you might not believe this, given everything I've told you about my own forgetfulness—but maybe this is a decision that my gender made without me.

You know, I bet my gender left me for someone else.

(This paragraph is a placeholder that can contain your decision that I deserved to be abandoned by my gender, since I was so inattentive to it. You would never abandon your gender, no matter how many miles you had to drive to retrieve it.)

(This space can hold the small ember of doubt that glows beneath your professed devotion. Would you really drive all that way?)

Now that I think about it, there was a waitress some miles back, in a diner where I stopped to stretch my legs and stretch my gender too. She was my mother's age, wore crooked eyeliner, and had a smoker's rough, rich voice and a nametag that said *Debra ;)*. She had a thin paperback in her apron, and I found myself guessing what it could be while I drank her strong coffee and ate the Texas Toast platter she set in front of me. I found myself remembering the various paperbacks I'd held in my own hands: *The Monkey Wrench Gang. Who's Afraid of Virginia Woolf? Three Lives.* And of course, *The Drunken Boat*, lost more than a decade ago.

Did my gender leave me for her? Maybe Debra is running fingertips over body parts that had previously held no attraction or interest—the soft arch of a foot, the curve of a deltoid—and discovering a fresh and foreign allure, even as other spots begin to feel alien and odd: tits and ass, for example, the old standbys. Is Debra fingering her nametag and wondering what might happen if she chose a different one? Is Debra testing out new syllables for pronouns, alien combinations of letters like ou, xie, za, per, aer. Is she waiting for one to suddenly swell with recognition?

I'm driving out of Kansas tonight. I'm already at its border, and in a few miles, I'll be somewhere else, somewhere new. I'm not very good at looking back, and even worse at returning to things and places I've left behind, but I wish Debra and my gender happiness and the joy of exploring new territory. If I come back to that small diner in that small town, I hope it will be as a welcome guest in the home my gender made without me.

(This is the last placeholder, where you can store your disappointment in this story, or your delight. This space can hold your comments and judgment, your boredom, or your revelation. This can be the space where you can look sidelong at your own gender, at the places where the two of you have sewn yourselves together, and where those seams might unravel, and what might spill out when they do.)

Volatile Patterns

Bogi Takács

Breakfast is miraculous – olives baked into soft sourdough bread, with mayonnaise and egg slices on top, yams cooked in savory sauce, and piping hot blackberry sage tea. My life-partner Mirun beams at me as I praise the food; it all came straight from the fabricator, but during our disastrous visit to Earth, e made sure we'd at least get some good food patterns out of the trip and constantly ran around with a handheld scanner.

"Each new planet strengthens the Alliance, awū Ranai." Mirun quotes the slogan only half-mockingly.

"And indeed," I say. We could use a break, though; the people of Earth have similar bodies to ours here on Eren, but their cognotype distribution is different enough to make interactions somewhat exhausting. And even today, our daughter Birayu woke us early with her cries that she wanted to go and learn from meni Abosana *right now*. At least meni Abosana showed up on schedule, Birayu's small study-group now happily off on a day of learning.

I sip my honey-sweet tea and try to relax.

Mirun bites into eir portion, drops and scatters pieces of egg on eir plate. E frowns and picks them up with eir fingers, drops them again. E looks all too tired, too, eir skin even paler than usual, eir small body curled up on itself in eir soft blue robes.

"I had a strange hypnopompic vision earlier," e says. "Quite violent. Someone dying. ...I haven't had any precognitive impressions in a while, but I haven't gotten much sleep in a while, either. May I show? It's intense."

I nod as e shares the memory reconstruction.

Fire – flames – scattered cries, someone down below breaking down a door. We need to get them out but where are they, this place was built before the new regs, how could it ever be compliant, who paid off who to get a permit? I can't think. I kick down a thin divider, it cracks under my boot, satisfying.

There are coatracks right inside, and they're all on fire, just like downstairs – there must be many separate sources, this is not an accident it is arson. I turn around and the coatrack next to me topples. I raise my arm to fend it off but the coats all fall out and on top of me, the angle is all wrong, the coats wrap around me to blanket me in flame and it should go out and my suit should be able to take it, but—

It's over, but my emotions will be reverberating for a while. Maybe I shouldn't have watched, but e is right about that particular foreboding sense of the future. I'm contemplating this when I get the call – highest priority, the emergency override passing through all my carefully set Do Not Disturb flags.

The caller has at least granted me the possibility to decline, but when I see his name, I know that we ought to talk. I pull my long overcoat around myself.

Commander Morosewi appears, standing next to our table, his body subtly translucent in that particular way that tells me it's an overlay. He's in the caverns of Ereni Security Headquarters, probably being video-recorded by his room, because when he sends his mental image of himself, he always wears a cowl in addition to his black uniform.

He glares at me, his pale skull – hairless in the Ereni way – glinting in the artificial light, his sizable jaw tense. The dagger-shaped tattoo on his right cheek and forehead twitches as he blinks.

He barks a greeting and I return it gracefully. Mirun murmurs something and he inclines his head toward em too.

Commander Morosewi always seems bothered by the sight of our tiny apartment. Is it because of the warm tones? The hand-carved wood and the blown glass? Certainly, these are indulgences, but Eren is no longer the resource-strapped former mining colony that it used to be.

"Much esteemed Ranai, head of the Iwunen household," he says – just slightly more formal than usual, but I am alarmed. "I'm here to ask for a favor. I know you've just returned from an investigation, but..."

I cross my thick arms – I know I can be just as intimidating as he is. "We've done enough for the Alliance for a few months at least. First the case with that dissident sculptor, then the trip to Earth..."

Commander Morosewi looks ill at ease. "This is not for the Alliance. This is for us. I am here on the express request of Supreme Councilor Orowōyā, and I defer to her expertise. She herself will take the time to tell you more if you agree."

Despite myself, I'm interested.

Mirun leans forward, forgetting about eir food. "Is this about the riots on Dehhe?"

Morosewi nods, eyebrows raised. "How did you guess?"

"I was just thinking, there aren't that many countries that Eren has relations with independently of the Alliance, and I read about the situation on Dehhe yesterday in my labor rights feed."

"I should hire you as an analyst one of these days," he says.

Mirun chuckles. "I don't think the esteemed Commander could hire me away from awū Ranai!"

The Commander clears his throat. "In any case, Dehhe asked for a team of investigators. They are having unexplained goings-on, and they suspect the riots are part of that."

"How will we be compensated?" Mirun asks the question that has been hovering unspoken in my thoughts. We have everything what we need – except for some well-deserved rest.

Commander Morosewi slowly turns around. "Dehhe has a longstanding tradition of blown glass that some say predates the times of the Old Empire..."

This is unlikely, I think, given that Dehhe was probably not even inhabited before the Old Empire, but my curiosity is tickled. "Do you by any chance have pictures?"

We finish our breakfast and I make a call to the Supreme Councilor. Orowōyā looks as resplendent as ever, the orange and crimson colors of her robe complementing the deep dark browns of her skin, the undulating, nonfigurative embroidered patterns gently promoting māwal circulation. Orange is for society, connections, ties that bind. Governance. One of the three fundamental colors of the Free State of Eren. Red is not fundamental, but important nonetheless: it's associated with power, this particular crimson tone referencing an inclination to subtlety over brute force.

We go through our greetings, comfortable in our formality. "I am truly glad you have agreed to this urgent request," she says and means it. I don't know her well, but we are on friendly terms – of all the Supreme Councilors, she is the most familiar to me.

"I don't know how much has Commander Morosewi explained?" she asks.

"Precious little, Councilor. He said that he deferred to you."

"Defers to me, or disclaims responsibility? Well then." She allows amusement to percolate through her features, but then she turns grim. "I myself know little. Dehhe is an important trade partner of ours, and I'm on good terms with Prime Minister Sounhha Sehisran. She said I could share this."

The Councilor gestures in the air and a recording starts playing; there is no video, just sound. Sounhha Sehisran has a soft, but vivacious mezzosoprano voice.

"– and if you could – I've been trying to regard all the misfortune as coincidental, but it's escalating, and some do suspect it's of a..." she hesitates, "magical nature. So far it's mostly been confined to the capital, but... it's starting to crop up in cabinet meetings as well, and I need to reassure my ministers, you understand. I myself am skeptical, but I defer to expert judgment."

Orowōyā waves away the recording and sighs. "All this deference in one day! I grow tired."

Every time we've gone outside Alliance space unprepared, things have gone badly. Now I know to ask a few questions beforehand. "Does the Alliance have any people on the ground?"

She grimaces. "They must do, but I haven't been able to get a contact – everyone is busy with the Treaty Enforcement scandal over there."

I wince. "I can see that. Eren is a small member state."

"Don't get me wrong, we have plenty of clout," she says. "I don't think they are deliberately withholding intelligence from us. It's just that Alliance Central is busy with its own problems these days. But if you could help us with this..."

I raise a hand. "Glass art goes a long way toward ensuring my cooperation."

The spaceport glitters; all too bright, all too white. I adjust my visual input just a little; Ereni standard interfaces have their advantages. The world becomes more bearable. Dehhe is rich, rich enough not to even consider joining the Alliance, and spaceports are locations where states like to showcase their resources.

Mirun spins around, trying to stare at everything at the same time. E topples over our floater-pod, yelps, scrambles up before I can step closer to help em. "Thank you, awū Ranai, I'm fine," e declares all too loudly. Over the years I've learned that *I'm fine* usually means impending disaster, so I nudge the floater-pod over to my side and firmly steer Mirun away.

I am explicitly awū, the dominant partner in our relationship, and this works out well for both of us. E relaxes a little.

We stand in line. Everyone else seems local. The people of Dehhe all have the same body template, like ours, but their cognotype distribution is more similar to that of Earth; our beloved Eren is somewhat of an outlier.

The officer who's verifying our hastily-issued visas is wearing a garish orange overcoat with embroidery and haphazardly sewn appliqué. The colors and patterns look as if they followed Ereni dress symbolism, but they don't – everything is off, as if I were hearing an unfamiliar language sharing a phonological inventory with a language I speak. The patterns don't make sense, but they *almost* do; the lines of the garment do not channel māwal in the right way.

When the officer takes our biometrics, I notice the scratches on her hands. Doesn't she have self-repair? I hope feral cats are not common here – I still remember my time in the Aruanar Combatspace.

I expect her to say something uncomfortable about our genders, interrogate us as to whether we are men or women, but she does nothing of the sort. She appears distracted, and possibly in pain.

Mirun messages me via our interface.

Awū Ranai, what kind of clothing is that?

I'm glad e noticed it too – being more observant of our environment is always handy when we are supposed to be investigating a crime. Except there is no crime, just general unrest, and politicians with ample strings to pull.

No one is waiting for us – our lodgings are just outside the spaceport, and we've been instructed to follow the red lines. Mirun runs around cheerfully and points out details that likely have no bearing whatsoever on our investigation. It's comforting that at least one of us feels capable of doing this after a trip across many jump points and a neverending flight on a passenger liner leaving Alliance space, while reassuring Birayu over video that yes, we will be back soon, and Anayāun-mowi will take her to the vegetable gardens in the evening.

The wave of raw emotion hits us in synch with the cold air when we step outside. We are swept away by the demonstrating crowd. The translation subroutines of my interface struggle with all the concurrent noisy input. Signs flicker from Ereni to Dehxen and back when I crane my neck around. I need to be back on Eren where my interface can rely on the local network – I need to be someplace else, very fast, because this chaos is the last thing I need right now –

"-say we can burn, burn, burn'em down–"

"Nem hagy-juk!"

"For the laborers, for the laborers! For life!"

"Solidarity means resistance! Kam defahi im–"

People of all shapes and sizes surround us. I don't know much about the local ethnoracial groupings, but I can parse out at least three different clusters. Everyone seems united in fury, running themselves ragged, their clothes torn.

I take a deep abdominal breath, pulling the smells of sweat and anger into myself. Exhaling them.

I strengthen my wards with the motion. Then I grab Mirun's arm – e's entranced by the crowd.

"Are these the riots you mentioned?" I yell.

"Awūn-ē, this is just a small demonstration –" e yells back, then the first large object whizzes past my ears, crashing into an advertising display. Sparks fly. The display screams "ENCHANTING EMBROIDERY!! SURPRISE YOUR SWEETHRRRG" and then it fizzles out. The crowd roars in unison.

"Let's get out of here before the cops show up," I shout. Fortunately for both of us, Mirun is skilled in much besides keeping tabs on labor rights activism in far-off countries. E pulls me down to a crouch, twists and turns, and in just three implausibly long steps, we are out of the clash. Mirun learned from me, but I couldn't have done this better myself.

We find ourselves standing right in front of another guard in a garish uniform, who stares at us and can only mutter "Magic."

Mirun shrugs. "Matter displacement. Or, technically, a shortening of distances. Nice to meet you?"

"You are the wizards?" the guard asks, oddly relieved. As his facial muscles relax, I notice a set of vertical scratches on his face and neck that end at his embroidered collar. "I've been looking for you."

The translation seems antiquated. "Wizards?"

"Magicians, witches. Bastard offspring."

I am about 99% sure the guard did not mean to say *bastard offspring.*

"We are the investigators from the Free State of Eren, yes." I don't think our specific terminology would make it across the translation gap, so instead of *māwalēni*, I just repeat what he said, with slight unease. "Wizards."

He's delighted, which is unexpected – in a language that has *magicians* and *bastard offspring* as distant synonyms, I would not expect to get a warm welcome. But cultural trends change fast.

"I'm so glad to meet you," he says. "I was sent to pick you up when the PM's office realized you'd be arriving in the middle of the newest demonstrations. You can drop your gear in your lodgings later, PM Sehisran is waiting for you."

Something must be really wrong if she's so ready to meet us. Mirun passes me a startled glance. But onward we go.

The officer steps back, greets the two other guards by the immense carved entrance to the PM's office.

Sounhha Sehisran hurries to the door to welcome us in herself, and my breath stops.

She is a short, stolid woman with round features, light brown skin the exact shade of mine, and wavy black hair that's chopped short just below her ears. She looks trustworthy in a way that probably makes constituents flock to her, but canny enough to lead an entire planet.

She is wearing a wonderfully intricate, richly embroidered, bright orange *Ereni* dress.

She notices my attention in the way of someone accustomed to it. "Oh, my dress? It was a personal gift from Supreme Councilor Orowōyā after the latest round of the trade negotiations."

And fitted to her personally, no doubt. It's not only a perfect size and shape, but I can also feel that all the embroidery and appliqué and cord serve to guide Sounhha Sehisran's natural māwal in a harmonic way. She would be charismatic without it, but with it, the effect is simply stunning.

I nod in appreciation, but also in mounting worry. "It's beautiful," I say. "Truly a gift fit for a ruler."

And appropriate, too – the designs clearly mark *the dress* as Ereni, but *her* as a foreign ruler. We have very delicate symbolism, and a tradition of gifting handicrafts to dignitaries, though they usually end up in a museum on display. I can't fault her for wearing her own dress, but it feels slightly like a faux pas, and I'm not sure why. Mirun also looks uneasy, but Mirun always looks uneasy, especially when we go off-planet. I need a moment to think this over, but PM Sehisran doesn't allow me a pause; not even to examine the majestic yellow glass vase on her massive desk made of solid wood, both designed in the style of quasi-organic abstraction.

"You will be able to accompany me to my next cabinet meeting, starting in just a few minutes," she says. "We can drink a cup of hot saba juice and then we must be on our way."

Mirun almost drops the cup that PM Sehisran presses into eir hands. E takes a sip gingerly, and makes a face – I know that feeling when self-repair tries to fix a scalded tongue. E valiantly downs the entire cup. I also taste mine – it's not so hot, but then again, my heat tolerance is very high. I'm thinking we might need it as PM Sehisran ushers us next door into a room full of shouting people.

The sight is astounding. In the spacious, eggshell-colored meeting room, there are about a dozen scratched and battered people, some even bleeding from small but fresh cuts. They are also wearing the most outrageous garments. Where the guards' haphazardly assembled costumes were simply garish, these are eye-gouging.

PM Sehisran smiles, embarrassed. "I seem to have started a trend," she says.

Mirun grins and messages me via my interface. *Awū Ranai, I do believe we've solved the case?*

I steel myself and message back. *We've solved the case, but yet again, we haven't solved the* problem.

When the ministers notice us, they jump to their feet, knocking against the oversize round table. An athletic-looking white man gets so close to me that Mirun holds out an arm to warn him off. He steps back, but continues yelling. "You need to figure out what's going on! You're the experts! We've been cursed!" He spreads his arm in desperation and his suit rips in half, showing his shaved and waxed abdomen.

I clap my hands three times to quiet the noise, and I put just a bit of māwal into the sound so that it would carry over the shouting. The ministers fall silent, but some are still so angry they are visibly shaking.

"Awū Ranai, if I may?" Mirun asks and I motion em forward.

"You haven't been cursed," Mirun says. "Your issue is simple and it traces back to the Prime Minister's clothes." E pauses, looks if they are following. There are sporadic nods around the table. "I'm also certain you could have solved it already if you deigned to ask your own experts."

"What experts?" a thin, dark-skinned woman asks, barely over her breath.

Mirun furrows eir brow and I know e's searching eir sensory logs for the exact word that would translate. "Wizards," e finally says.

Another round of yelling erupts.

PM Sehisran slaps her palms on the table. "Enough. You know I am a skeptic above all. I don't care what the Ereni do, and how they explain it, but they are the experts."

A skeptic? Note the word choice, I message Mirun. This planet is not such a low-māwal area to allow plausible skepticism. *Have there been fluctuations in māwal levels recently?*

Mirun responds: *The Alliance should have that data on file if they really have people on the ground, but we don't. Still, that would be a reasonable guess.*

"Allow me to explain," e says to PM Sehisran's cabinet. "These garments are carefully designed to guide the wearer's... magic, if you will. The lines and patterns are not arbitrary. Improvising on them

36

without being aware of the design principles is... not going to be fruitful."

I also step in, seeing an opening to tie the abstract to the personal. "Do your clothes scratch you when you put them on, take them off? Do they tear? Do the zippers catch at your skin? Do your wounds not heal?"

Nods around the table.

I cede the floor to Mirun again. E goes on without missing a beat – we work well together. "You all tried to one-up each other and have the most gorgeous design approximating the Prime Minister's garments, but the clothes work well for her not because an Ereni artisan has gone overboard with embroidery, but because what there is works well with her natural magic. You are locked in a positive feedback loop, a runaway reaction where the more and more dramatic your garments, the more likely you think they are going to increase your station, but instead the more havoc they cause. Without you even realizing." E sighs. "These patterns work. Their distorted versions also work – and produce further distortion."

I wonder how much of this made it across intact with our imperfect translation software, but whispers and half-sentences start up around the table. "Then the riots?" "They did start in the textile industry..." "The burning factories?"

I pounce on the words. *"What* has been burning?"

Mirun gasps as e connects the dots. "But of course! The factories – many clothes with the same patterns, and combined with an atmosphere of grievance – your workers aren't paid that well, are they?"

A minister stands, pulls herself up to full height, shaking with anger. "If you are accusing us of sweatshop labor –"

This isn't going to end well. I raise my hands. "No one is accusing anyone of anything. But for now, it would be best if production of these... garments could be halted. For purely safety reasons."

"These are private-owned enterprises we are talking about!" a man yells and slams a fist on the table. "We can't just shut them down with what, riot police?"

I also raise my voice. "If you don't shut them down with riot police or whatever else you have, you might need to shut them down with firefighters and emergency medics. What has burned down already?"

PM Sehisran grits her teeth and looks away, probably accessing her interface – I'm not sure what is standard on Dehhe.

Then she hisses softly; then she curses.

"I can't send this to you, some kind of incompatibility," she says and steps to a wall. "But I can project it."

We see a tall, cuboid building, with tiny windows that explode outward as we watch. A deep voice comments. "That's not glass. That's heat-resistant plastic."

A minister asks, "Is this ongoing right now?" PM Sehisran nods, mutters agreement.

The minister who's still standing whispers, "This should not be happening."

"Do we have a video feed from inside?" I ask.

The deep voice says, "I have some from a helmet cam."

With my feet rooted to the floor, but hopelessly unrooted on this foreign planet, I watch as I see the familiar images play out: a bulky firefighter raising her arm as a flaming coatrack topples on her and the suits twist and bend around her, trying to suffocate.

The feed cuts out.

"There are still firefighters inside – and workers," the deep voice explains. "All the equipment outside is broken. They can't get the jets working."

I snap my head to Mirun. "We need to ward it. All this disturbance..." I don't need to explain. We are

39

working on it already, reaching out with our minds across the distance. It doesn't seem very far, actually.

"Where is this place?" I ask. "How fast can we get there?"

PM Sehisran smiles drily and a wall rolls away. Behind it there is a set of floor-to-ceiling glass panes, and beyond that is the capital; smoke rising in the distance.

"I've always wanted a good enough reason to do that," she says.

Mirun glances out, eir mind half-occupied by the warding. E speaks slowly. "I'd rather not fly, we need all our energy once we get there. Maybe a ride?"

PM Sehisran is confused for a moment, and I know she didn't realize at first that we can fly under our own power if we must – there is enough ambient māwal for that, but just barely. It's a stretch. And right now we can't be thinly stretched, if we want to make any difference. She nods.

"I can offer my own transport. I've always wanted a good enough reason to do *this*, too," she says as a vehicle descends – probably from the roof – and hovers by the windowpane. PM Sehisran slides away the pane and steps into the transport. There is no wind; there must be a force field around the building, the vehicle, or both.

I gently guide Mirun into the transport – eir focus is at the building site.

The standing minister yells. "I'm also coming! I'm the Minister of Infrastructure, I need to be there!"

I get the sense there must be some kind of rivalry between her and Sounhha Sehisran. It's not my concern.

"Come then," PM Sehisran says with just a touch of weariness.

It takes just a few minutes for us to arrive, speeding across the evening sky, toward the sinking sun. The building is already assailed by jets of water – our wards have taken hold, and the firefighting equipment is operational again.

Mirun shakes eir head to clear it for the next task. I must go in – ostensibly to gather evidence, to convince the skeptics. Honestly, I just want to make sure we get the remaining workers and firefighters out. I have never been afraid of being burned, and I have more than enough māwal to keep harm at bay.

"You can help me sustain my defenses," I say. "From *outside*. This is not an argument."

E nods. We hug, we kiss. Then I run into the factory, my power hastening my steps. The ground floor is occupied by rows upon rows of broken fabricators, and I pass them quickly by, make my way upstairs where the more valuable handmade garments are produced. I run into storage room after storage room, open a cabinet only to have half a dozen garments fall on me, try to attach themselves to me, bounce off my shields.

This is not going to help. How am I to carry them? I make the back hemisphere of my shield sticky and throw the flailing garments into the air. I run again, a wobbly layer of clothing behind me. I've been experimenting with making my shields spin, as a form of active defense, but I need to keep my field of view clear of flapping shirt-arms and unraveling threads of embroidery.

I dash into a larger hall, full of fabric in a large, roiling, sparkling heap. If there is a critical mass of angry māwal-active objects, this is it.

I roar like a bear, my shout shaking the air, and the fabrics separate, scatter against the walls. The ambient māwal calms down a little. The sparks subside. I take a deep breath and send the last few minutes of my sensory stream to Mirun outside – we need a backup in case something goes wrong. Because of this boneheaded need for *proof*.

Behind a door, in another hallway, I find the unlucky firefighter trapped under the rack. She does not seem badly burned, but she's unconscious and will not rouse. I drag her up and back across corridors upon corridors. Anger fuels my strength. All this could have been avoided. All this.

Outside, I hand her to the emergency responders, then without losing speed I turn to PM Sehisran and her circle of onlookers. "You want proof, I'll give you proof!" I yell and shoot straight up into the air, drawing on the raw strength of the flames, my own anger and that accumulated in the garments, from frustrated and tired and annoyed and fuming and raging laborers, urged on by supervisors desperate to fill the sudden demand for the newfangled foreign fashion.

I rise, spreading my arms.

I soar past floors upon floors of chaos, land on the roof. A small group of people are trapped up there, waiting for a rescue. Where *is* the rescue?

I ping Mirun and e shouts at PM Sehisran until the ministerial transport takes to the skies again, and I watch as the last of the begrimed, soot-covered laborers and the bone-weary firefighters stumble into the pristine interior of the vehicle. I can't help feeling glee, a rare emotion, and a feeling of justice being done – even as I know that the interior probably has enough nanites to gobble up and reprocess an entire truckload of soot in a matter of minutes.

PM Sehisran will get a great photo op out of this.

I can't sense anyone else still in the building, but I ask Mirun to make sure, before I spread my arms out again and jump.

It must be the anger clouding my mind.

I misjudge my power.

My smooth glide turns into freefall.

My eyes lock on PM Sehisran as her mouth opens in a desperate scream. I shouldn't see such small details from so high up, but I do.

It must be the fear.

"Awūn-ē!" Mirun shouts and pushes me upward with a burst of raw māwal. My robes and all the ravenous garments I'm still dragging behind myself billow out toward the sky.

It's not the smoothest landing, but I manage.

"Are you satisfied?" I groan at the prime minister's entourage. Mirun trundles toward me on unsteady feet. We hold each other close for a long moment before we separate again, for my turn to yell.

"If you wanted safe patterns, you could have asked! These are formal, ceremonial garments!" I point at PM Sehisran, then sweep my arm back in an arc and disable my shields. The clothing items plop to the ground in time to punctuate my words. "*These* are misguided imitations."

Mirun adds, "You will want to destroy them quickly."

I sigh. "And hire a Cultural Interchange team next."

PM Sehisran glares. At this moment I realize that there are many ways of creating a position ruling an entire planet, but very few of them are peaceful. Even if she's doing her best. Even if she was elected to her position. I don't know the history, but I know power and I know temptation.

I push my excess anger into the pile of clothes and turn around to watch the sparks take to the air from the impromptu pyre.

I cough and turn back to PM Sehisran.

I must calm myself.

"I believe we were discussing traditional glass art," I say.

Birayu looks at the yellow glass vase, its soaring arcs and undulating lines pitch-perfect in the style of quasi-organic abstraction.

She tilts her head to the side and frowns.

Objects hold their histories, and I'm wondering what she senses; then she turns around and marches back to the fabricator to make a set of six rainbow cupcakes.

Island, Ocean

Lauren E. Mitchell

The topmost room of the lighthouse is given over to the vast hot lamp that illuminates the sky from dusk until dawn. Below that is the watch-room, where the great cans of fuel for the lamp are arrayed around the walls, and the lighthouse keeper's desk and chair sit facing out to sea. Her logbook is filled with precise small handwriting: observations on the weather, the stars, and the names of the ships that pass her tiny, rock-toothed island safely by.

Below that is the music room. Its door mostly stays closed; the blue paint is softened and faded by dust. There's a saxophone and a clarinet and a cello. She can play none of them; her instrument was always the piano, but who brings a piano to a lighthouse? No, these are an artefact of those who came before her, and she keeps telling herself that she should clean the room out, but she never does.

Her bedroom comes next. It's the only room where the windows are permanently shuttered, for her night runs from dawn until dusk and the sunlight not only permeates her eyelids, but overheats the room in the summer months. She has a big bed for just one person, spread with a handmade patchwork quilt, a thick warm one in the winter and a thin one, almost as thin as a sheet, in the summer. In summer she lies very still and has difficulty sleeping, thinking of the oil cans overhead, wondering if they will stay safe and sealed and not overheat and combust. In winter she curls into a ball under the quilt and sleeps soundly, the wail of the wind a curious lullaby. There's a tiny wardrobe built in along one curve of the wall where she hangs her succession of plain white t-shirts and plain blue jeans. At one end there's a thick windbreaker, but she's grown used to the rain and the wind and rarely wears it. She does wear a shapeless woollen hat, though, not so much because of the weather as because her grandmother knitted it for her. It is the same rainbow clash of colours as the quilts.

The last room above ground level is the storage room, lined with racks of canned food, freeze-dried food, and other supplies designed to last as long as possible. The supply boat comes once every six weeks from the mainland with fresh fruit and vegetables; the lighthouse keeper makes them last as long as she can. It also brings letters from home, and she makes those last as well, averaging the pages out over the nights until the boat is due again, writing her replies as she reads through so that when the boat returns she has the envelopes ready.

The ground floor is almost empty. Though tiny, the island is not flat, but nonetheless the waves can still rise up to engulf the ground floor, and after losing two good pairs of boots to the water the lighthouse keeper has learned not to keep anything in it. Yet it is not entirely empty; an intricate mural, coloured square by square, marches around the walls, each square a month in the life of whoever tends the light. There is a neat white square between each succession of squares, with the name of the previous keeper and the dates of their keeping written in the centre. The current keeper has quite enjoyed filling out her squares with the paint kept in the storage room; hers are mostly pictures of the flowers and plants that cling tenaciously to cracks in the rock, unlike the merfolk and sea-monsters and shipwrecks that are dotted throughout the earlier rows of images. She has always admired life that survives in unlikely places.

She rises at dusk and sleeps not long after dawn; it's one dawn long into her keepership when, going down to the shore to check her crab traps, she at last meets a merfolk.

They have pulled themself ashore from whatever undersea kingdom it is that they inhabit to lie on the little beach between the rock formations on the eastern side of the island, where the tide pools are biggest. Their head is pillowed on their arms, their hair a damp tangle of curls the same golden colour as the early morning waves burnished by the rising sun. Their skin is a lighter shade of pinked gold that could either be a tan or just the way that the sunrise hits their skin. At first she is afraid that they are dead, but as she cautiously steps closer she can see the rise and fall of their breathing. They're lying on their stomach; their spine curves gracefully down and their hips flare out, but then there's another inward curve and instead of splitting into two legs their lower extremities are fused together in a graceful, pearlescent tail. Their scales are patterned coral-red and anemone-orange, and the fin at the end of their tail shades from pink to purple like the inside of a pipi. They splash it lazily in the lapping waves. Her crab cages lie empty beside them.

There's only one thing that she can think of to say, and that's a simple, "Hello?" Her voice is rusty from disuse.

Their head snaps up from their arms and they look up at her, green eyes wide and fearful. They start to scrabble backwards on their elbows into the foam.

"Wait!"

Surprisingly, they stop, rolling from their stomach to their back and sitting up. Their chest is caked with gritty sand that does little to cover the small smooth swells beneath it. Their neck is smooth save for two thin gill slits on either side of their throat, closed over as they sit on shore. A neatly braided beard hangs golden from their chin, threaded with shells and pearls. The beard extends up their cheeks as little more than damp fluff, meeting their hairline alongside ears with little seahorse frills. Another tuft of gold bristles over their upper lip.

"Hello," they say carefully, and then, "I ate your crabs."

She looks at the empty cages. "Oh."

"I'm sorry," they offer.

"I—it's all right. I can catch more." She tucks her hands into her pockets and watches their curious gaze rove over her jeans and boots. She can't blame them for staring; she's staring just as much, trying to focus on their tail rather than on anything else, like the triangular patch of darker scales she can't help thinking of as being between their legs, though they have no legs.

"I've never seen you before." She says it at the same time as the merfolk.

Their laugh is truly bubbly. "I don't usually come to shore here, but the crabs smelled good." They diffidently brush some of the sand off their chest, utterly unselfconscious, and she can feel the beginnings of helpless arousal stirring in her. The sand catches in the downy hair that starts at their clavicle and arrows down between their breasts, petering out just above their navel. In places it glints red or orange instead of gold, like coral. She can't keep from looking. 'They're harder to catch further out.'

"You don't trap them?" She hunkers down, hands on her knees.

"Oh, we do, but the crabs are bigger." They make a gesture encompassing a shell the size of a dinner plate, claws the size of their small hands, and wince. She thinks of steamed crab with hot butter, eaten in the topmost room looking out over the darkness, and knows that's not how it is for them.

"How do you live down there?" she asks abruptly. "Isn't it too cold and wet?"

They think for a moment and then shrug. "Not when you're used to it. How do you live up here? Isn't it too hot and dry?"

"Not when you're used to it," she says, and they share another laugh, as though this is a perfectly ordinary conversation. When they laugh the delicate flaps on the sides of their neck flutter a little. Then, when they brush more sand off their front, she sees the fine webbing between their fingers, stretching between the second knuckles. They catch her looking and lift their hand to press it against hers.

She expects clamminess, the cold of the deep sea, but instead their skin's just pleasantly cool on her palm, like a drink of fresh water on a warm day. Their hand is smaller than hers but she can see from the muscling of their shoulders and upper arms that they possess a good deal of physical strength. They must need it, to be able to swim against the tide, against the pressure of the ocean.

For a moment their fingers intertwine, and then the merfolk pulls their hand away.

"I should go," they say, and rolls adroitly sideways into the salty sea foam.

"Wait!" she calls after them. "Will I see you again?" But they have dived beneath the waves, vanished into the deep, a sunbeam gone into darkness.

She sighs, stands up, and picks up the crab traps to rebait and reset, if not for herself, then in the hopes of luring them to her shore again.

"You taste like the sea," they say, lifting their mouth from her.

She hasn't the breath to reply, lying half in and half out of the waves like a drowning sailor washed to shore, but it's not her gasping mouth they've been applying theirs to. Her clothes are scattered somewhere above the high tide line. "Like oysters, or lost copper pennies."

She still can't respond. They laugh and slap their sunrise tail against the water, splashing them both. "You're like a squeezed-out sponge."

This draws a reaction from her at last; she rolls onto her side and begins to stroke their hair, carefully combing the ever-present tangles out with her fingers. She says nothing, but she knows that she does not want to be a sponge, simply soaking up their presence and the pleasure that they bring her. They nudge their head against her hand and she draws them closer. When they kiss she can taste herself in their mouth. She doesn't know if she does taste like the sea, the way that they claim; it seems to her that the taste of the sea is what's left in their mouth once every last trace of herself is gone.

One night, as the sun sinks below the horizon, she goes down to the water where they usually meet and they are not there. She waits as long as she can, but the lamp must be lit and there is no sign of them.

It's only when she finally walks back up the shallow, seaweed-encrusted steps that she sees them. She doesn't know how she missed seeing them on the way down, but perhaps she was hurrying, heedless of what was at her feet thanks to her anticipation of what would be on the beach.

They are huddled about halfway up the steps, skin gleaming coldly in the moonlight. The first thought that strikes her is how pale they are all over, how much of a contrast this is to their sunlight self.

The second thought, which should have been the first thought, is that they have legs.

Their feet and ankles are striped with blood. They are breathing normally, but the fine slits on the sides of their throat have vanished. She lifts them into her arms and then is torn whether to take them up to the lighthouse or back down to the sea. At last she chooses up, carries them step by step to the solid front door, which stands open, waiting for them. The mural stares at them with dozens of faces as they enter the ground floor room and she kicks the door shut behind them against the rising whistle of the wind.

She is still uncertain whether this is right or wrong, but she takes them up the spiral stairs anyway, stopping in the storage room to rinse the blood from their legs. They stir a little in her arms when the cold water hits their skin, but does not wake. She cannot see any cuts or wounds on their feet; there is no visible reason for the blood, but it is streaked a long way up their legs and her imagination fills in the details.

A cosy bed is a strange place for a merfolk, but it's where she puts them, tucking the quilt around them and fluffing one of the pillows under their head. She feels guilty about leaving them there, but she has to tend the light; it is full dark now and the ships will be sailing regardless of whether she has a visitor. She goes up the last spirals of stairs, past the music room door, to the lamp room. The wind makes it chilly, but she ignores the cold, lighting the lamp and feeling the space heat instantly. It's a rare night that she has to do anything but sit here, but she makes sure the fuel reservoir is well-filled and that there are no specks of dust on the lamp's glass to block even the smallest ray of light. Once she has done all that she goes back downstairs to her bedroom.

They are sitting up against the pillows and watching the door. Their eyes are unfocused but retain their green clarity. Horribly, she thinks that their expression must match that of drowning victims in the seconds before death glazes their eyes right over. She opts not to share this comparison with them and just sits down beside them on the bed, reaching for their hand. Even the webs between their fingers have vanished; this transformation, whatever has caused it, is extraordinarily thorough.

Their eyes focus on her when she touches their hand. It's a vast improvement over the vacant stare. They smile and touch their throat, and then their lips, and then shake their head.

"I don't understand," she says, but she is afraid that she does.

Their brow furrows in frustration and they repeat the gestures, this time with a rougher gesture across their lips. She doesn't know what to say to their muteness and then it doesn't matter anyway because they silence her unspoken words with a kiss, fervent and deep and needing-wanting-hungering.

They have always met in the shallows between their worlds; this is a chance to show them the comfort of her bed, instead of sand and stone.

"Should we do this? I don't want to harm you," she says.

They give her an impatient look, and guide her hand to their breast, and she loses all desire to protest when this is so clearly what they want. She sets about learning their body anew, touching and caressing those places that were closed and scaled and are now open: warm, wet, hard, soft. They make no sound but the arching of their back and the flexing of their muscles tell her all she needs to know, not to mention the way they gather her hair in their hand when she goes down on her belly between their legs, smiling up at them before lowering her face to them.

And now she knows the true taste of the sea. It is dark and secret and deep and she wants to throw herself into them and drown.

She lifts her mouth from them and then rises from the bed to unlatch the shutters, pulling them open. The light that flashes out across the sea powerfully illuminates the bedroom; she can be certain that it has not gone out.

But when she returns to the bed and to them, before long she can see nothing but them and their body entwined with hers. She can feel only the way that they move beneath her, above her, with her.

It is a long, long time before they sleep, curled together under the quilt. She latches the shutters again but she feels certain that the light will not go out, not on this night. The sound of the waves far below lulls them to sleep even in this strange place and she is not far behind them, listening to their breath, their chest rising and falling like the ebb and flow of the water.

As always she feels the dawn in her bones. Usually she is looking out to sea when the sun first peeks over the horizon, but not this time. She opens her eyes and slips out of bed to open the shutters again, letting the first light into the room, and then hurries quietly upstairs to turn out the lamp. She stands for a minute looking out; the sky is a leaden grey and the wind has whipped the waves into a frenzy, but despite this she is cheerful. They will find ways to communicate, and she will care for them, and she will no longer be alone. Solitude is a way of life that suits her, but it is growing harder to appreciate the longer that she knows them. She casts one last look at the ominous low clouds and then goes back down towards her bedroom.

As she passes the closed music room door, she heard the soft, mournful strains of a funeral march begin.

The clarinet is unbearably sweet-sounding. The saxophone should be too cheerful but somehow isn't, sounding like the keening of the gulls that often circle the tower. The cello weaves the two together. And it is impossible for all three to be playing, because there is nobody in the lighthouse except for herself and the merfolk. Besides, how would a being of the sea know how to play any of the instruments?

She jerks the door open angrily and sees all three instruments sitting in their dusty cases, just as they always have.

A sudden fear seizes her, and not because she is the kind of woman given to believing in ghost stories or anything of that sort. She slams the door shut and pelts down the remaining stairs to her open bedroom door, but not fast enough to escape the resumption of the music, which is decidedly *not* music to her ears.

The quilt has fallen to the floor. They lie on the bed, their face once again too pale, shining tail slapping against the stone and shedding scales. She runs to their side, seeing the final seconds of the transformation completing itself; the gills open again on the sides of their neck.

They are harder to carry in this form, but she lifts them anyway, taking the stairs two at a time and kicking the door open against the wind. The steps down to the beach are slippery with wet seaweed and kelp thrown up by the tide; she takes them recklessly, painfully aware of the merfolk's almost non-existent breathing.

She can't get to the bottom of the steps; the waves have risen to the high tide mark and beyond, foam spuming up another yard beyond that. She is hesitant to just let them go into the maw of the sea when they are in this state, but is unsure what else to do.

The solid rock outcropping to her left catches her eye. She hastens back up the steps and walks out onto it. Every footstep is sure and steady despite how treacherous the surface is. She stands at the edge of the drop with them in her arms and looks down at the ocean roiling below.

If the merfolk are real, will the sea monsters be real as well?

They fall together in silence. The water opens to accept them both with barely a splash.

The supply boat comes when the waves die down and the island is safe to approach once more. It brings fresh crates of food, and a new lighthouse keeper.

She enters the lighthouse with trepidation and then feels it fade away as she sees the mural on the wall. While the man brings in the crates from the boat, she stands with her hands linked behind her back and looks at the paintings. The oldest ones are dull and dusty; she makes a mental note to wipe the walls down, maybe touch up some of the more chipped areas, when she's got time. The newest ones are so fresh they could have been done yesterday, although the island has been abandoned for a week.

The last picture is a fascinating work of imagination; a merfolk and a woman, poised above the sea in mid-jump. Below the waves glitters a fabulous palace.

She wonders if she will ever find out what happened to the former lighthouse keeper and thinks it's better if she doesn't.

In the meantime, she has a lighthouse to tend... and a painting of her own to begin.

Author Interview: Lauren E. Mitchell

Lauren E. Mitchell lives and writes in Melbourne. I caught up with them to talk about their story 'Island Ocean', NaNoWriMo, and future plans.

"Island, Ocean" is based on "The Little Mermaid". Was that where the idea for it started? What made you want to rework this fairy tale in particular?

In this case, the key was the 'transform' part of 'transformative work'. I had a lot going on in my own head regarding gender identity, so the idea of writing something where there was bodily transformation involved but still nothing that strictly defined my merfolk as a specific binary gender appealed to me. Plus it meant I could drop in a couple of references to Paul Jennings's short stories, specifically 'Lighthouse Blues', and anytime I can do that it makes me happy.

Are there other works of fiction you've enjoyed reading that explore diverse gender identities?

One of my favourite gender diverse characters is Nico from Rachel Gold's novel *Just Girls*. Nico is genderqueer as heck and goes by a few different pronoun sets during the course of the book. I like Mira Grant's ongoing inclusion of nonbinary characters in her works. But I think one of my absolute favourites has to be Vaarsuvius from the *Order of the Stick* webcomic. V's an elf who is alternately referred to as 'he' or 'she' depending on the perception of the character talking about them, and is married with children... who refer to V and their partner Inkyrius as 'Parent' and 'Other Parent'. It's only recently that I truly realised how much that made me identify with V—even more than the purple hair.

If you could own any item of fictional technology, what would it be?

A teleporter. It would solve a lot of my mobility access issues and save me my daily two hour round trip commute. Plus I'd be able to get places I can't access on public transport. The downside would be if it turned out to work as well as any of that kind of technology on *Red Dwarf*, where it usually needs a bit of percussive maintenance to get it going.

I had a great time completing NaNoWriMo last November, and I'm in awe of everyone who helps make this huge month-long event happen. You have a couple of different roles - can you tell me a little about what you do and some of the highlights of the experience?

I'm the Municipal Liaison for Melbourne, so I run some events and coordinate others over the course of the month – a kick-off picnic, a whole lot of write-ins, and a weekly social catch-up. Every year it's a little different, because some people come and go but others stick around, and I love fostering the sense of community support. There's just such a huge amount of creative energy that springs up starting in October when we have plot-ins and carries right through to December.

I'm also a volunteer forums moderator; my particular assignment is the LGBT+ Fiction forum, which is now two years old and which I've been working hard alongside the NaNo staff to make as positive and functional as possible.

Lastly, what's on the horizon for you? Tell us about any forthcoming publications, works in progress, or anything else you'd like to mention.

At present 'Island, Ocean' is my only forthcoming publication, but I'm working on a couple of pieces for open submission calls: one is for a poly anthology through Less Than Three Press, which I'm excited about because I have a previously published poly piece with them and I'm planning to revisit those characters. I'm hoping to make it super adorable while also looking at the characters' families, their respective attitudes towards the relationship, and how those attitudes are changing the deeper the triad's commitment to one another grows. Even if I don't get it done in time for the deadline, getting my head back into that universe will be good practice for going through all the bits and pieces of writing I have for it and putting them together into some sort of linear narrative.

Sandals Full of Rainwater

A.E. Prevost

Piscrandiol Deigadis clutched the battered suitcase close, jars rattling inside as the train whined and staggered to a halt. Piscrandiol waited, eyes shut tight, feet and elbows pressing in all around them as passengers rushed for the exit. Over the din of disembarking, the rain made itself insistently known on the steel roof of the car.

The rain had started sixteen miles back, well beyond the border that separated Piscrandiol's native Salphaneyin from Orpanthyre. It had begun as a mist and crested to a deluge, and it had cracked Piscrandiol's life wide open like a miracle. Piscrandiol pressed their palm against the cool glass, heart pounding. Every trickle of water on the other side ghosted a kiss across their skin.

It had not rained in Salphaneyin for so long.

Orpanthyre was a city of rain, a city where no one went thirsty and anyone could find work. The storm battered against the tarred roof of the train station like a thousand shouted promises as Piscrandiol waited for the exodus to subside. Finally, Piscrandiol took a breath, adjusted their skirts, and stepped out onto the platform.

The street outside the station was a noisy jumble: handcarts and chickens and babies, sunken-eyed miners, families struggling not to lose sight of each other in the heaving human tide. Copper roofs covered the downtown sidewalks, patina battered by seasons of rain, which traced elegant green arcs against a backdrop of stone and wood. Piscrandiol let the flow of the crowd lead them away from the station.

Despite the roofs, there was water everywhere: splashed up by carriage wheels and the jostling steps of strangers, pouring out of the rumbling and broken-open sky, rushing down cast iron eavestroughs and churning white in the grate-covered gutters by Piscrandiol's feet. It was an excess, an exuberance of water, enough to fill every well in Salphaneyin. It sloshed through Piscrandiol's sandals and weighed down the hem of their skirts like it had nowhere better to be.

Piscrandiol braced themselves against a stone wall at a crossroads where the crowd thinned out, and forced down a breath, eyes closing for a fluttering moment of reprieve. In just a short while, they'd reunite with their cousin Geluol, who'd left for the city three years ago. There would be a meal, a roof, a bed. All Piscrandiol had to do was keep their feet moving towards Seven Ingot Three Homeshare, and then the ordeal of traveling would be over.

"If it's an umbrella you need, you've certainly come to the right place."

Piscrandiol's knuckles turned white on the handle of their bag. They turned to the source of the voice – tall and ruddy-tan, with elaborate clothes, standing beside a narrow cart hung with dozens of colourful umbrellas.

The stranger graced Piscrandiol with a businesslike smile. "New to the city?"

Piscrandiol nodded, years of Orpan language classes tumbling together and screeching to a halt in their mouth.

"You'll need one of these – get you started right. Salphaney, aren't you? Lots of you coming 'round these days."

Piscrandiol nodded again. They could feel the blush seeping into their cheeks, volunteering all the information their words couldn't provide.

The umbrella-seller smirked. "Look, I've got a nice blue one that matches yunna skirt. Fifteen lam."

Piscrandiol's mind stumbled over the pronoun – first gender, if they remembered right, but was it

Piscrandiol they saw that way, or themselves? Piscrandiol had encountered the concept of gender at school, of course, when they'd studied the Orpan language with everyone else, but having it thrown at them in conversation shattered six semesters' worth of confidence.

Piscrandiol shook their head. "I'm sorry," they managed, handing over a few coins before the umbrella seller could say anything else. "I'm sorry." They grabbed the umbrella and hurried back into the crowd.

The homeshare turned out to be a broad, four-storey square of dark tarred wood that flanked an open central quadrangle, with a custodian's office at the front. Rainwater pooled on the floorboards around Piscrandiol's shuffling feet as they tried to take in the fact that they were being turned away.

"Not moun fault we're full up, child," the custodian was saying, round brown eyes watching Piscrandiol like a clock ticking down to the end of their patience. "There's a lot of you, coming into Orpanthyre. Not even just you Salphaney people, either. There's fires in Mollend, flooding downland..." They shook their head, dark coils tumbling about their shoulders. "I don't want to turn yeym out, but there's no room here."

"But... but makes no sense," Piscrandiol said, trembling slightly. "Please, I – I need to see my cousin. Geluol Bibenia?"

The custodian rapped sturdy fingers on the top of their desk. "Bibenia. Wait half a minute, Bibenia. Hiy's the one been called out of town, isn't hiy. Left a message. Wouldn't be for yey, would it?"

Piscrandiol sighed, letting their eyes close briefly. Out of town? "Probably."

"Well, I can't read Tisalpha, but here. I presume this is for yeym then."

The custodian handed Piscrandiol a flat metal container, and they accepted the familiar weight in their hands with some relief. Popping the latches revealed a hastily-imprinted clay tablet, its workmanship unmistakeably Geluol's.

Babyhead, work beckoned & when the work calls I go. Sorry I couldn't be here to welcome you good & proper. We'll catch up when I get back – mining gig's usually 2-3 mo. but then I'll buy you dinner promise. Bunch of dinners. Anyhow if you need anything ask Dolein, they're good people & saving keys to apt. five-four for you. Stay tough. – Dumdum

Piscrandiol couldn't help but smile at the childhood nicknames, but the idea of spending two or three *months* in the city without anyone they knew made the room spin. They closed the case and looked at the custodian. "When?"

"The message? Oh, week ago, maybe. Was it for yeym?"

Piscrandiol nodded, placing their hands on the desk to steady themselves. "Who is Dolein?"

The custodian's patience cracked, a humourless smile carving dimples into their smooth cheeks. "Me."

Piscrandiol put down the first month's rent, effectively handing over most of what remained of their savings, and walked into the quadrangle past a busy jumble of sheds and tarps that suggested a vegetable garden and chicken coop. They dragged their suitcase up four steep flights of indoor stairs, legs trembling and aching, and turned the key in the latch of apartment five-four.

Piscrandiol let the weight of their suitcase pull them through the door. The empty rooms echoed the drumbeat of rainfall on the roof immediately above, a hollow sound that trickled into every corner of the space. Piscrandiol wandered to the window and cracked it open, letting the downpour rage against their outstretched hand. They put it to their lips and drank; they splashed rainwater on their face. This was real. This was home.

Well, not quite yet. Piscrandiol carefully opened their suitcase. With all the jostling, they'd feared the worst – but the only casualty of the trip was one aloe leaf, snapped off and oozing. The jars themselves were all intact.

Relieved, Piscrandiol unfolded the trellis against a wall, hanging the hoops straight. The heavier jars went on the bottom, of course – cloudy glass packed with earth and life-giving moisture. Piscrandiol spoke gently over each of the succulents, fingertips soothing leaves and stems, tiny petals, squat bulbs. In the topmost jars, thin, fleshy tendrils of dark blue spread out, banded with luminescent rings that cast a soft fairy-light against the wall – glowweed, Piscrandiol's favourite. *Now* this was home. Whatever came next, just like the plants, Piscrandiol would lay down roots and thrive.

The tendrils' gentle glow wouldn't light the whole apartment, though, and a search through closets and corners came up empty of candles. Piscrandiol steeled themselves in the bathroom mirror before trudging back down the stairs to face Dolein.

The custodian's office was unexpectedly busy. Two road-weary travelers were in heated conversation with Dolein, while a third tended to a small child; a second, older child crouched off to the side, playing with a bit of wire.

"But I'm telling youm we wrote ahead," the tall knife-faced one said, black hair clinging damply to their collar. "Weeks ago."

Dolein pursed their lips. "And *I'm* telling yiym we don't have record of it."

The traveler's barrel-chested companion tugged at their downy beard thoughtfully. "Gislen, if the letter got lost, there's nothing we can do."

"Like hell there isn't. I'm not letting min family rot in the damn rain."

The third adult hoisted up the toddler, offering Piscrandiol a timidly apologetic smile. "I'm sorry, were yey wanting to speak with the building manager?" They eased one long, ink-dark braid away from the child's grabbing hands. "We're in a bit of a situation, I'm afraid."

Piscrandiol shook their head. "I have arrived here today," they said, as if that would explain anything. Classroom sentences snapped apart and melded with others. "I wish to get a candle. For upstairs?"

"Oh, I think we have some," they said, setting the toddler back down. "Outside, though, in the cart. Appi, go play with Tafis, okay?"

The toddler hid their face behind the adult's knee, clinging to the trouser fabric with needy hands. Piscrandiol smiled, lightly, and shook their head. "I can wait."

The tall one, Gislen, walked over to lay a hand on the braided adult's shoulder. "We'll work this out, Annat," they said, voice gentle. Their black eyes took in Piscrandiol. "Hello," they said. "And you are?"

"Hey lives in the building," Gislen's friend said, before Piscrandiol had a chance to embarrass themselves. "Hey're looking for a candle."

"Oh, we have those," Gislen remarked.

Piscrandiol blushed. "I can buy," they insisted.

"Nah, we've got this." Gislen's smile made them blush more. "Refe and Annat can handle the housing muddle; I need some air anyway. Come on."

The tarp was fastened securely to the pull-cart, but Gislen seemed to know the exact location of everything underneath, because it took them mere moments to yank out a fat yellow candle and hand it to Piscrandiol. Piscrandiol thanked them earnestly.

"Not a problem." Gislen rocked on their heels, glancing over at the water spout gushing nearby. "You're from Salphaneyin, right?"

"You can tell?"

"The way you speak," Gislen said, offering Piscrandiol a quick smile. "Nothing wrong with it to mim. Hear you're having quite the drought, right? We're from downcountry, opposite kind of problem. Fields are washed out. Family decided to give it a go in the city."

"Twenty years," Piscrandiol said. "I think. The last time it rained, I was baby."

Gislen frowned, nodding sympathetically. "Rough. Well." They barked a laugh. "Got all the rain you could possibly want here, I guess."

The one with the beard burst through the door. "Listen, shou's being a goddamn hardass— oh hello," they said, noticing Piscrandiol. "Refe Eibas Suu." They shot out a broad hand to shake. "Gislen bothering you?"

Piscrandiol giggled, shaking Refe's hand. "My name is Piscrandiol Deigadis, how do you do. Gislen is very nice."

"Oh, I *see*," Refe grinned pointedly at their companion. "Anyway, not that I wish to interrupt, but— Gis, yi've got to try talking to this person. Shou says they're full up, offers such kind sympathy for the children, of course, but says there's *rules*, Gis, including not renting out an apartment contracted to someone else. If yi've ever heard of such a thing."

Gislen chuckled, shaking their head. "Love, I've spoken all I can to that one. Unless Annat has some tricks up shun sleeve, I think we're at an impasse here."

Something compelled the words out of Piscrandiol's throat. "I—" Both travelers turned to look at them, and they continued, face burning. "I, ah, you can stay with me. Tonight. Your family. I have big space, a-and small things."

Gislen pushed the hair out of their blinking eyes. "We couldn't do that. Put youm out like that."

Piscrandiol shrugged. "The weather is very bad."

"Yeah, it is." Gislen admitted. "I mean… if Annat can't work something out with the building manager… You'd really do that?"

Piscrandiol shrugged again, smiling.

The custodian wouldn't commit to the safety of leaving a pull-cart in the quadrangle, so Gislen and the other four members of the Eibas family, with Piscrandiol's help, lugged everything up to apartment five-four. Appi, the toddler, ran to the plants immediately; only Refe's reflexes saved the trellis from disaster, scooping Appi into their arms, where they squirmed and reached towards the droopy glowweed.

"That's a pretty plant, isn't it, Appi," Refe said. "We don't want to hurt it, right? So don't touch." They turned to Piscrandiol. "Nothing in there that would hurt a child overcome by curiosity, is there?"

Piscrandiol shook their head. "Maybe, if… if Appi decides to fill the belly with rocks and dirt… it could be problem, but the plants? They will not make sick."

"They really are beautiful." Refe grinned. "We're very honoured you invited us into your home tonight, Piscrandiol. We'll pay, of course."

Piscrandiol shook their head. "No, no," they said. "You… your childs – children, they should not be in the rain." They blushed. "Ah, you also should not be in the rain, but…"

Refe laughed, a warm sound that shook their stomach. "I understand. Don't worry about it. We really are thankful."

"Let us provide supper, at the very least," said Annat, carefully putting a metal-cornered crate down on the floor before taking Appi from Refe's shoulder. "We have enough to share."

"That would be nice," Piscrandiol answered, smiling. "Thank you."

The meal was sausages fried on an elaborate stove that Piscrandiol would not have known how to light, along with apples, dry bread, and cheese. Piscrandiol brewed a hot, sweet tea from a bundle of dried herbs, which garnered compliments even from the children. That evening, the Eibas family laid out their mats in the main room and slept in a pile, Tafis and Appi tucked among their three parents. Piscrandiol smiled at the scene of familial comfort, but declined the generous invitation to partake, explaining that they preferred their own mat. They wished the Eibas clan good night and retired to the nearby bedroom.

Piscrandiol laid a thin wool blanket on the floorboards and stretched out on it, listening to the rain. They felt guilty for lying about having a mat, but the companionship in the living room wasn't theirs to enjoy. It should have all been different. It should have been Geluol offering candles and dinner and friendship, not the warm pile of strangers snoring outside of Piscrandiol's door. Geluol, their only family in Orpanthyre; Geluol, who would be gone for months.

Piscrandiol rested their palms against damp eyes, shoulder blades digging into the floor. No one here even spoke Tisalpha; no one knew the same stories or laughed at the same jokes or loved the same food. But going back to the drought and hunger of Salphaneyin… No. Their parents were counting on them to send money home. Their parents were counting on them to thrive.

The grey light of dawn teased Piscrandiol's eyes open from an almost-sleep of fears and memories. They rolled onto their back and let out a soft breath.

Piscrandiol stretched their aching bones by the tall narrow window, watching the world turn slowly golden in the sun. At some point, during the night, the hammering rain had stopped; Piscrandiol rested their forehead on the glass, and watched layer after layer of Orpan architecture reveal itself as the day burned away the lingering mist. It was a beautiful city, really, this foreign place, when there were no people to ruin the view: verdigris domes and wrought iron swirls, tarred wood, green glass, smoke drifting from the factories downwind. A city built for rainy days.

Piscrandiol sighed and headed into the small bathroom, taking a quick wash before changing into clean clothes. They shaved carefully in the plate-sized mirror, taking time not to miss any patches in the corners of their jaw, and brushed the tangles out of their waist-long hair.

"Scrandle?"

Piscrandiol smiled, looking down to the source of the brave attempt at pronouncing their name. "What is it, Appi?"

"Nanat says, Na, Nanat says breakfast is ready." The toddler hopped from one foot to the next. "I need to poop."

Piscrandiol laughed and let the child take over the bathroom, heading out into the living room where Refe was stirring a thick white porridge on the stove. Their sleeves were pushed up, their hairy arms tattooed in bright blues and pinks and greens.

"Just in time," they said, smiling. "It's a sunny day in Orpanthyre. The rarest of miracles."

Piscrandiol glanced out the window. "This is sunny?"

Refe laughed loudly. "I like yunna sense of humour!"

Piscrandiol smiled shyly and busied themselves with making tea. It had been so easy, for a time, to completely forget about the Orpan concept of gender. Of course avoiding pronouns forever would have been too much to hope for.

Studying Orpan at school, they had run up against its dizzying array of pronouns – three genders with three grammatical cases, a system that at least made up in consistency for what it lacked in common sense. Memorizing the words had been work, but not nearly as hard as understanding when to use them. The teacher had tried to explain the concept of gender: a way the Orpan people spoke and presented themselves differently, based on some sort of internal social sense of being. In class, some had gossiped behind chalk-dusted fingers that gender was about what Orpan people had between their legs, but the teacher had overheard and categorically denied it; whatever it was, as far as Piscrandiol was concerned, it was as inscrutable as how bats flew in the dark.

Watching the Eibas family communicate over breakfast, though, with their effortless and ever-shifting palette of pronouns, made Piscrandiol feel clumsy and wrong. For one thing, it didn't even seem like the words people used always stayed the same. Annat said *heym* to refer to Refe, while Gislen said *hem*. Where Gislen called Annat *shum*, Refe said *shumma*. Whatever gender the Eibas clan saw themselves as having, it changed depending on who they were talking to, leaving Piscrandiol scrambling after clues in the context. It all seemed needlessly complicated for something that, as far as Piscrandiol could tell, didn't mean anything at all.

After breakfast, Refe helped Piscrandiol with tidying up, drying each plate as best they could. "I hate to ask, but the little ones were on their feet all day yesterday, and... Well, is it all right if I stay here with the children while Annat and Gislen go look for somewhere else to stay?" They frowned, a crease puckering their brow. "I'm very sorry to add to the burden we've already placed on you..."

"No, no." Piscrandiol shook their head quickly. "No burden. Please stay." The thought of suddenly being alone in a bare apartment with only the plants for company opened a yawning pit of dread in Piscrandiol's stomach. It wouldn't even be so bad, really, if the Eibas clan stayed a little longer.

Refe was charming and warm, and gestured expansively when they told stories, which happened a lot. The children made a game of exploring the apartment, which allowed Refe and Piscrandiol a quarter hour of storytelling before the toddler was back at the trellis of succulents.

Piscrandiol stood up quickly, but Appi's sibling was already carefully pulling the little one away from the fragile plants. Piscrandiol gave them an appreciative smile.

"Um, Piscrandiol?" Tafis said, squinting at the jars. "Why'd you carry all this stuff with you from Salphaneyin? Gis said you didn't even bring candles."

Piscrandiol looked down, chuckling a little. "Well, ah, hmm. For us, every plant has meaning, has useful. All from my family home in Salphaneyin, but at home," Piscrandiol said, gesturing broadly, "the whole wall. We can stay cool, and – look," they said, pointing to the dip between two fleshy leaves, where moisture was collecting. "We can… ah... A system, it takes water from all leaves and puts together for drink."

Refe walked over. "That's amazing."

"Why don't you just collect rainwater?" Tafis asked, frowning in a sharp way that suddenly brought out the resemblance to Gislen.

"It doesn't rain in Salphaneyin, Tafis," Refe explained.

"Like, at all?"

Refe shook their head. "Right, Piscrandiol?"

Piscrandiol nodded sadly. "Twenty years, almost, no rain."

"Wow," Tafis gawked, looking towards the window. "That must be *amazing*."

Refe laughed and rubbed the child's feathery black hair. "You need rain to make food grow, Taf. And to drink, and clean things, and all that. –Appi, what's that in yenna hand?"

The toddler quickly hid something behind their back, but not before Piscrandiol recognized it.

"It is broken leaf," Piscrandiol said quickly. "I put on window side yesterday. Not dangerous. Good for sunburn."

Refe crouched down in front of the toddler. "Give it to me, honey."

Appi scowled and shook their head.

"I just want to see it, okay? Come on. I'll give it back."

The child hesitated, then grudgingly handed their parent the snapped-off succulent. Refe stood, sighing. "Definitely chewed on."

"Not dangerous," Piscrandiol repeated, reassuringly. "Also…" They indicated a low, moss-like plant with tiny yellow bulbs. "This one, for when you have stomach hurt. Very good, even when small child eats things."

"But this stuff looks really heavy," Tafis said, prodding one of the jars. "Annat said we couldn't bring anything heavy. I had to leave all min best toys."

Piscrandiol's fingertips traced the ridged edge of a leaf. "Heavy, yes," they mused, wondering how in the world they could express in Orpan what the trellis meant to a Salphaney family. "Heavy but… this one," they said, reverently lifting a small jar with sharp, red-tipped leaves, "it is cut from… very old plant. Many generations. And this one, I found in desert. I was about same old as you." They indicated a bubbly little spray of light green. "All here, these are from kitchen of house when I was a child, and – ah! This one," Piscrandiol quirked a smile, showing a coral-blooming cactus, "is ah, how do you say, farewell? Farewell from my first sweetheart." They grinned. "Do you see?"

Refe hoisted Appi into their arms. "Yeah," they said, smiling softly. "I do."

"I don't," said Tafis.

"Some things," Refe said, "you carry around with you no matter what, because… Well, maybe they're heavy, but they lift you up, too, right?"

Tafis tugged on Refe's sleeve. "I don't get it."

Piscrandiol turned to the window, smiling, blinking back tears.

Maybe it was the influx of refugees fleeing the devastation of the floods, or Salphaney filling train car after train car, but when Gislen and Annat returned that night, they proclaimed there was not a single available apartment in the city. Piscrandiol grinned from where they sat on the floor, hair twisted into loops by Appi and Tafis, and made the offer they had been thinking about all day.

It was surprisingly easy to agree on the division of rent and chores, easy to accompany Annat to the market to invest in sleeping mats and lanterns, cups and rice and soap, the many necessities of family life. Piscrandiol spared a little for clothing, as well: no one in Orpanthyre wore skirts, since there was always a gutter or a drain for them to get sodden in, so they brought a pair of simple tan trousers, and boots that sealed the water out. Annat taught Piscrandiol how to pull their copper-brown hair into two long braids, flat and skinny down their back; it took hours to get it right, leaving Piscrandiol perplexed by the apparent ease of Annat's deft brown fingers to do the same, but in the end the braids received the Appi tug of approval. Annat laughed with delight.

Annat was also the first to find employment, carding cotton at one of the city's sprawling mills. Things were looking hopeful for Piscrandiol, as well: they were on the mill's waiting list, and would be contacted as soon as a position opened up. Refe, who spent most days out in the city seeking work, told Piscrandiol that if they'd made the list it was best not to continue applying elsewhere, so they ended up shouldering most of the home and childcare duties with Gislen, at least until the family could afford to send Tafis and Appi to school. This suited Piscrandiol just fine.

One morning over a cup of tea, as the children practiced their letters in chalk on the floor by the window, Piscrandiol asked Gislen about Refe's work.

"Heh's a professor, by training," Gislen said, shifting comfortably on the floor cushion. "History. There must be a hundred unemployed professors of history in Orpanthyre, of course, but heh's dead set on finding work in hen field."

Piscrandiol looked up from the dewflowers the two of them had started sketching with a bit of the children's chalk. "It is not good?"

"I mean… Sure, I'd also love to work in my field, but instead, I'm answering every 'help wanted' sign I see. I don't blame Refe, really I don't," they said, running a hand across their forehead with a sigh. "Heh's *good* at hen job. But we can't feed five people – six," they smirked warmly at Piscrandiol, who blushed, "on one person's salary. We'll barely make next month's rent, in this… What." They narrowed their eyes. Piscrandiol was laughing.

"You…" Piscrandiol shifted a bit closer, reaching out to brush the smudge of chalk from Gislen's brow.

"This." They raised a chalky fingertip before dotting it playfully on the tip of Gislen's sharp nose.

Gislen laughed and grabbed Piscrandiol's hand, and Piscrandiol's heart rioted in their chest.

Gislen's eyes were black and bright like galaxies, long straight lashes casting flickering shadows over flushed clay-dark cheeks. Gislen's fingers laced with Piscrandiol's tightly, and Gislen's lips… They were soft, hungry, and hot and bitter like tea, and Piscrandiol never wanted the kiss to end.

Appi shrieked something at their sibling, and Gislen and Piscrandiol parted, far too soon. Piscrandiol's heartbeat throbbed against their interlaced fingers. Piscrandiol could barely dare presume – barely had the words to ask – if this was all right, but in the way Gislen held their hand, in Gislen's irrepressible smile, Piscrandiol seemed to understand that the Eibas family would approve. They rested a flushed cheek on Gislen's shoulder and watched the children play.

It wasn't much later that Gislen found work at a butcher shop, and Piscrandiol was left to look after Tafis and Appi alone. Gislen came home every night tired and smelling of blood; Piscrandiol heated water for their bath and regaled them with tales of their day.

And when the children slept, there was time enough for the two of them.

"I hate waiting list," Piscrandiol sighed, limbs tangled with Gislen's, blankets kicked to the edge of the mat. "Annat doesn't even need to say anymore. Just comes home and looks sad."

"Something will open up," Gislen said, kissing Piscrandiol's temple. "Refe seems to think so."

Piscrandiol made a quiet noise. "Refe is a good friend. Sometimes, ah, many times, I worry about jealous... About us... "

Gislen smiled. "Very considerate, but you don't need to worry. Refe thinks you're great. You know that, Pisc."

Piscrandiol tucked their head under Gislen's chin. "I... I don't think I... I'm attracted," they admitted.

"To... Refe?"

Piscrandiol nodded, but looked up sharply when Gislen laughed.

"Oh, that's hardly what I meant. It's not like you're expected to – to be attracted to all of us. Refe never thinks about that stuff, anyway. I mean, it happens sometimes." They grinned. "Or else we wouldn't have Taf and Appi, but..."

Piscrandiol smiled, looking down awkwardly. "Oh, ah, about that, I won't… I mean… When we…"

Gislen nuzzled Piscrandiol's hair. "You're not going to get me pregnant, no. I'm being careful." They stretched happily. "However, I do know that Annat's been thinking about having another baby, so if you're interested…"

Piscrandiol sputtered, and Gislen laughed, muffling it with a pillow. "I'm kidding. Shou *has* been stealing glances at you, though," they said, thin lips drawn into a smirk. "Shou thinks you're adorable but is much too kind to express jealousy."

Piscrandiol tucked their blushing cheek against their lover's arm. "Well, ah, *shou* can, ah, talk to me about it, at some time. I would be happy to know shou better."

Gislen laughed, twining their fingers together. The sound filled up Piscrandiol's heart with light like a balloon.

"All right. That's fine by mim. But… it's not *shou*; for you, it's *shum*."

Piscrandiol squinted, still flushed. "I …Sorry?"

"*Shou* likes *youm*, *you* should talk to *shum*," Gislen said. "Is it okay if I explain?"

Piscrandiol sighed. "You … Orpan has much too many pronouns."

"We don't have that many! Anyway, I haven't wanted to correct you, but you should probably say *yiy* to me instead of *you*, actually."

Piscrandiol grabbed the pillow and smacked Gislen with it. "It is difficult!" They complained. "We have four pronouns; Orpan has forty-five."

Gislen wrestled the pillow from their grasp, grinning. "Fairly certain you have more than four."

Piscrandiol counted irritably on their fingers. "Okay, well, then nine. It is still not forty-five, Gislen."

Gislen smiled, tossing the pillow aside. "I love the way you say min name," they said, and pulled Piscrandiol into a kiss that made them forget about words entirely. It was unreal, finding such brightness in the grey of Orpanthyre's endless storms. Under Gislen's tenderness, their hunger, Piscrandiol unraveled like an abandoned skein.

Just when it seemed the rain would go on forever, the season fizzled into something hotter and hazier. The air hung yellow in the evenings; the streets were loud with the buzzing of insects, and blossoms in a riot of colours burst out on the trees. And one heavy, humid day, Refe came home jubilant, arms full of sweets and flowers.

It was a part-time position, Refe was quick to qualify, a teaching assistantship for a single course that was hardly their specialty, but the faculty at Five Rosewater College had seemed happy to take them on, and they would start next week. It was a trek, on the far side of town, but with the additional income they'd finally be able to send the kids to school. Tafis ran around the apartment in glee, and their little sibling followed suit without really knowing why, hands full of candy.

The following week, Piscrandiol walked Tafis and Appi to Ingot City School, and found themselves alone in Orpanthyre for the first time in nearly two months. As they wandered towards the vegetable market, it was hard to ignore that they were the only adult left without a job; the only member of the household, even, without a place to be. Back at the homeshare, Piscrandiol chopped parsnips and chard and hot green peppers for stew. Two months on the waiting list at the cotton mill. Two *months*. It was impossible nothing had opened up. Unless there wasn't one at all; maybe "waiting list" was just a way to let Salphaney off easy without actually giving them employment.

Piscrandiol slammed the knife into the cutting board.

Geluol hadn't trained as a miner. Their cousin was a poet, a painter, who had woven worlds of beauty onto the best pottery from the family kiln. But Orpanthyre had robbed them of that gift. Orpanthyre had thrown them in a pit full of sweaty, aching bodies and demanded coal. And Geluol was one of the lucky ones; lines stretched along the sidewalk at the day-labour agencies, Salphaney skirts and sandals and unbraided hair, and very few Orpans between them.

Piscrandiol would never get off that waiting list.

They took a deep breath. How could they explain this to Annat, whose eyes held a steadfast shimmer of hope, whose little heart beat so fast in the darkness? How would the Eibas family react, hearing that the city that had welcomed their kin had no mercy for the stranger? The hospitality of their people was tarnished, but rejecting it would paint Piscrandiol as ungrateful.

Piscrandiol's stomach churned with dread. The Eibas clan had been so kind. They could never know.

Every day Piscrandiol visited the vegetable market, and every day they pushed through their awkwardness and asked the merchants if anyone they knew was looking for help. It shouldn't have surprised them that no one ever was. It shouldn't have surprised them that the 'help wanted' signs had all been taken down from the shop windows. It shouldn't have surprised them that by the time they made it to the day-labour lines after market, the jobs for the day were already taken, or that the factories weren't hiring. Every day, Piscrandiol went home filled with grey thoughts, and sought solace in a trellis full of plants that had adjusted far better to Orpanthyre than they had. And every evening, the Eibas clan came home full of stories, and Piscrandiol served them soup and let them talk. No one seemed to notice Piscrandiol's silence and secrets, and Gislen still shared Piscrandiol's sleeping mat, sometimes.

It was so easy to pretend that nothing between them had changed, so tempting. Piscrandiol should have known that Gislen saw through the silence. That they would wait for the middle of a quiet night to bring it up, catching Piscrandiol unwound and vulnerable.

"Is there anything we need to talk about, Pisc?"

It wasn't even a reasonable secret to keep. It was taking up all this space between them and it was pointless – a tangle of shame and worthlessness, a weight of unbelonging. Why couldn't Piscrandiol just let it go?

"Talk to me," Gislen pleaded. Skinny fingers tangled in Piscrandiol's long hair.

"I talk every day," Piscrandiol snapped, pulling away. "I... I talk every day at the market." It was like pruning away what they were too ashamed to share, working to shape a palatable fact. "Every day... every day I speak Orpan until I have no words anymore." The sculpted truth filled Piscrandiol's gut with bitterness.

Gislen sighed. "I'm sorry. I wish I spoke Tisalpha... Maybe you could try teaching the children."

Piscrandiol closed their eyes. "Maybe. I'm so tired. Everything is *shou* this and *yunna* that, and every person knows well how to say it, but I..."

"You'll get there." A hand reached for Piscrandiol's shoulder.

Piscrandiol shrugged off the touch and sat up. "I don't know." They swept their hair off to the side, locks clinging together with cooling sweat. Nothing ever dried in Orpanthyre. "I can't... how am I supposed to *know*."

Gislen sat up beside them. "Your gender? You just do. You don't need to overthink it."

"You – *yiy* just do," Piscrandiol retorted. "Annat just does. Refe just does. Maybe Appi even. I just *don't*."

Gislen sighed. "I'm sure you do, Pisc. Listen – maybe I'm wrong, but you... you're more like Annat than Refe or mim, right? It's not like you can *not have* a gender. Maybe, I don't know, youn culture and min culture present it differently. But—"

"Our culture doesn't present it at *all*, Gislen," Piscrandiol said, glaring at them. "Why is this so hard to understand? We don't think, 'Oh, I am this, that person is an other this'. Some behave this way, some behave that way, but it is not *gender*."

"Pisc, I find it seriously hard to believe that youn entire region doesn't have anyone with gender in it." Gislen rubbed at their forehead.

"Well, I – it doesn't matter what yiy think! I'm sick of – of always being *youn* and *shou* and – I don't want it!"

Gislen tried to take Piscrandiol's hands, but they pulled back.

"All right." Gislen's hands hung in the air. "All right. I can use different words, love, I can... Just tell me what you want."

Piscrandiol ran a hand across their face. They were having an argument, now, and none of it was even the point... Except that it was. Just one more way in which Piscrandiol was an outsider. "It... Yiy're kind, yiy're so kind, Gislen," Piscrandiol murmured, voice dull with exhaustion. "But... It is everywhere.

Everywhere I go, I – I can't get away, everyone looks and *assumes*, one thing, another thing…"

"I can't change society, Pisc." Gislen clutched at the blanket. "Even if you don't feel it, you… What can I say? You give people a certain impression. It's just how we work."

Piscrandiol stood and left, naked feet scuffing across the floor to the living room.

"Pisc…?"

Piscrandiol didn't listen. Ignoring the sleeping family, they stood on tip-toes to grab the pruning shears from the top of the trellis before returning. Gislen gasped and took a step back, but Piscrandiol ignored them too, heading for the bathroom.

"What are you doing? Please, I'm sorry —"

Piscrandiol looked straight in the mirror as they lifted the shears. Two feet of stringy red-brown hair fell to the floor like dead leaves, like shed skin. They heard Gislen gasp and stifle a cry, but did not stop until their head felt weightless, untethered. Then they put the shears down on the sink, and looked up.

Gislen was weeping.

Piscrandiol shivered, their shoulder blades catching the chill of the night air. "All it said was lies," they said, feeling like they should cry as well, but finding tears too distant to answer the call. "All these pronouns are lies. So now? Am I different pronouns now?"

"I…" Gislen took a careful step closer, then another, finally pulling Piscrandiol into their arms. "I don't know," they said. "I don't care. I love youm. Yem. None of it, all of it, forget it. Forgive mim. I'm sorry. We'll figure this out. It doesn't matter."

Piscrandiol stood in the resolute affection of Gislen's embrace, until, with time, they stopped shaking.

The children spent the morning grabbing handfuls of Piscrandiol's new short hair, getting it to stick up in ways that made them topple over laughing. Piscrandiol knew they should find some way to speak with the adults about what happened, address the rift that was slowly taking form. But the silence stretched out through a day and a night of missed opportunities, and then Tafis came home from school with tiny sprouting peas and asked Piscrandiol for help planting them, and Piscrandiol found it far too easy to focus on that instead.

The quadrangle was crowded with summer-rich gardens, and among them, waterlogged and flecked with moss, Piscrandiol found the patch of soil dedicated to apartment five-four. They spent a morning on their knees in the mud, Tafis eager to help, until the sprouts were nestled in grooves in the fresh-turned earth. Piscrandiol showed the child how to hammer together a frame to help the pea shoots grow tall, and the two of them went out every day to watch the tender green vines reach for the sky, until they grew strong and thick with sweet-smelling flowers.

The garden was a revelation. Little by little, through the days of planting and weeding, Piscrandiol found their spirit returning. Appi surprised them with a shriveled piece of taro that had sprouted long hungry tendrils – a cherished toy, which they'd been hiding somewhere. Piscrandiol and Appi planted it together, reverentially, and it soon spread broad, heart-shaped leaves that thirsted for the sun. Piscrandiol bought seeds from the market to keep it company, traded with neighbours, and even brought down a fat little blockleaf succulent from the trellis upstairs. Soon the garden was flourishing with watercress and climbing spinach, and Tafis' vines had sprouted pods of fat peas that the children scarfed down by the handful. In time everything grew, even hair.

Or, almost. One morning Piscrandiol found the blockleaf sagged and wilted, drowning in the sodden earth. Piscrandiol kneeled at the edge of the plot and dug their trowel into the soil, carefully lifting the plant up. Rot was spreading in its shallow roots; but maybe if they kept it in a pot, with holes in the bottom…

"Cousin!"

It took Piscrandiol a moment before they realized that the deep voice had spoken in Tisalpha. They turned just in time to be swept up in familiar sinewy arms and spun around as if the mud on their knees and the plant clutched in their hand didn't matter. They stared up into a grinning umber face.

Geluol was back.

Piscrandiol's cousin hit it off immediately with the Eibas clan, talking easily about everything and nothing, and also talking about Piscrandiol, which made them want to disappear. Annat insisted they have a special supper, and Refe ran out to get a whole goose already roasted while Annat and Gislen fried vegetables and Tafis tended the rice. Piscrandiol threw together a salad of garden greens and stumbled through their cousin's giddy questions. Had they gotten the tablet; had Dolein helped them out? How had they met the Eibas family and ended up living with them? Did they have a job? Were they seeing anyone? Piscrandiol tumbled through replies in a mother tongue that felt clumsy until it didn't, and suddenly they had their own voice again.

And Geluol… Geluol was perfect at Orpan, too, navigating pronouns like all of it was a breeze, like they'd always known how, like gender was the simplest thing in the world. Watching them all chat over tea in the lamplight, with Appi falling asleep in their lap, Piscrandiol wondered when Geluol had become more of a stranger than the rest of them. Piscrandiol stroked Appi's ink-black curls and stared into the lamp's flickering flame.

The next morning, before they could change their mind, Piscrandiol pulled Gislen aside. "I've been lying to you."

Gislen frowned and cast a glance over their shoulder where Annat was dressing the children. "What?"

Pisc tucked their hair behind their ears. "For a few weeks. I'm sorry."

Gislen glanced away again, then took Piscrandiol's hand. "Let's go outside."

Pisc nodded. Their hand felt cold and clammy inside Gislen's all the way down the stairs.

They stood on the covered walkway outside their door, sheltered from the light rain.

"What's going on, Pisc?"

Piscrandiol watched the rain trickle down the taro leaves. "I've been looking for work."

Gislen turned and looked at them. "Yeah?"

Piscrandiol nodded. Thunder rumbled, but distant.

"And?" Gislen said, encouraging. "Did... did something happen? Did you find something?"

Piscrandiol bit their lip and shook their head.

Gislen took a deep breath. "So... what, uh, what have you been lying about?"

Piscrandiol glanced over. "Annat... Annat believes the waiting list, and Refe said, I mean, Refe said I shouldn't look, and... I don't think the waiting list is real, or, not real for *me*, and..." They took Gislen's hands, looking up into their gaze. "You all work so hard. But no job wants Piscrandiol. So many Salphaney looking for work. So I... I make soup, and I grow vegetables, and every day I look for work, but there is no work. And my parents, I need to send money, and you, your family, I take advantage. You are so generous, but this city, I can't always..."

Gislen gently squeezed their hands. "Oh, love," they murmured, tugging until Piscrandiol was in their arms. "Oh, love."

Pisc closed their eyes, cheek on Gislen's shoulder. Gislen was quiet for a good long time, and Piscrandiol hung on, scared that when they let go, Gislen would say something terrible.

"You're not taking advantage of anyone, Pisc," Gislen said, finally. "I love yem. We *all* love yem. The children think you are the greatest thing they've ever met."

Pisc chuckled, in spite of themselves, and gave Gislen a squeeze.

"Listen," Gislen continued, parting enough to be able to meet Piscrandiol's eyes. "I'm so sorry if we gave yem the impression you... you shouldn't be looking for work because Annat put yem on a waiting list. You can do whatever you want. And we're *happy* having you at home, if that's what you want. I didn't realize we were putting this pressure on yem. I know we didn't mean to."

Piscrandiol smiled weakly. "Yiy're mixing up pronouns," they pointed out. "First and second."

Gislen blushed, grinning. "I'm trying something new. Adapting."

Piscrandiol took Gislen's hand back, threading their fingers together. "Geluol has no trouble with pronouns," they complained.

"So what." Gislen kissed Piscrandiol's head. "Some people behave one way, some people behave another way, and that doesn't mean anything, right? That's what you told me. I believe it."

Piscrandiol leaned their temple against Gislen's shoulder and looked out at the garden. The peas were all but harvested, their vines growing tough, but the season was far from over. It would be time to plant something else soon.

Author Interview:
A.E. Prevost

A.E. Prevost is a Canadian writer and linguist. We talked about writing, language, and travel.

Could you start by telling me where you got the idea for "Sandals Full of Rainwater" from?

So I'd been mulling over some story ideas about immigration and belonging for a while, and then the call for submissions for this anthology came up, and that immediately made me want to nerd out and do something ambitious with pronoun systems... But what really made it all come together was, I was out at dinner with my friend Grace Seybold, and she was telling me about how she was prepping for a move out of town. She had a bunch of succulents that she wanted to bring along, but instead of bringing the whole plant, she was taking careful cuttings and arranging them in jars in a suitcase. That just was such an amazing mental image for me that the rest of the story kind of unfurled around it – this idea of what you bring with you, and what can be nurtured and thrive when circumstances change. I asked her if I could use the jars idea in my story, and she said yes!

Orpan has forty-five pronouns. I've been wondering since I first read the story how comprehensively you created this aspect of the language. Did you have a spreadsheet of all forty-five? Did you choose them almost randomly to give a sense of a complete system? Something in between?

Haha, yeah, I actually had a whole chart set up at the back of my document that I kept referring to! Tisalpha, the protagonist's native language, has no gender at all – grammatically as well as socially – and just uses *they*, so that was straightforward enough. But Orpan culture has like, this three-dimensional gender space in which you situate yourself in relativity to someone else, according to these three separate gender axes that I deliberately never name or define, because I didn't want to think in terms of "male" or "female". But yeah, in Orpan, your perception of yourself and others is what determines which pronouns you use for yourself and for them. So since it's already a pretty different way of looking at things, I didn't want the pronouns themselves to seem too jarring to readers. I wanted them to seem kind of English. So I went back to Old English and got some inspiration there. Anglo-Saxon had three genders and multiple grammatical cases, so there was a lot of material to work with! Orpan ended up with three cases itself, so in the end I had this 45-pronoun chart and also a little diagram with doodles of the different characters and how they viewed their genders in relation to each other, to make sure I used the right ones. It was a lot of fun.

You're a linguist, and that background has had an obvious influence on Sandals Full of Rainwater. Can you tell me a little about how that influences your fiction writing in general?

It's weirdly hard for me NOT to work language stuff into my stories. Just like it's hard for me not to do gender stuff. Those are just both universes that keep pulling me in, that I can never understand well enough and so keep coming back to. So language actually tends to be an important part of worldbuilding for me. How you talk about stuff can say a lot about the priorities and prejudices of your culture, and there's no reason in speculative fiction that those should line up with any particular society in the real world. So I like to put some thought into that, and I think my training as a linguist gives me a whole toolbox for it. We take a lot of language stuff for granted, we often just assume that our way of saying things is the default. But language is so alive and diverse and adaptive. I'd say the number one skill linguistics taught me is to question my assumptions and embrace variation.

Were there any other works that influenced this story?

I think I got some indirect emotional inspiration from the work of Rose Lemberg, that I had just gotten into at the time. There's a care and gentleness and hope to their work that really resonated with me, and I was like, *yes*, more of this please. I love writing stabby action adventure, but their work made me want to write warm and compassionate stories as well. I think it's just so necessary to carve out a place for gentleness.

Are there other works of fiction you've enjoyed reading (or watching) that explore diverse gender identities?

I've only recently been discovering stories with nonbinary protagonists, actually. I think the first one I read was *Lizard Radio* by Pat Schmatz, which hit me right in the gender feels. Also, I just absolutely devoured *Mask of Shadows*, by Linsey Miller. Seeing all these nonbinary identities portrayed on the page is sort of exhilarating, even if I don't think I've read a story yet with an agender protagonist... Unless you count Ann Leckie's *Imperial Radch* series? Maybe that's part of why I love those so much!

If you could go to any real place in the world, and any fictional place, where would you go?

Oh wow, hmm! Well for real places, I'm not kidding, I'd probably pick New Zealand. I've always wanted to visit and it just seems so beautiful there, but it's so far away from Canada. I lived in Japan for a couple years and almost figured out a way to visit New Zealand from there, but it didn't work out. Now, a fictional place is harder, hmm... I might have to pick the Wayfarer, that super awesome found-family ship in Becky Chambers' *The Long Way to a Small Angry Planet.* The galaxy has some scary things going on, but if a crew like that had my back, I'm sure I'd be fine. I just love how healthy a lot of the relationships are in that world, and I love the quiet focus on mental health and self-care and rest and giving each other space. I think I'd be pretty okay. Plus, you know, spaceships!!

Can you recommend a short story and a novel to readers?

Short story: *Waiting on a Bright Moon* by J.Y. Yang. It completely drew me in with its lush and vivid worldbuilding – I can still clearly picture a lot of the scenes and places in my mind, months later. It's about love and singing and oppression, and it's just this beautiful queer Chinese space opera. I also loved how some of the passages, the songs especially, are in untranslated Chinese. I imagine this could add a whole layer of depth to the story for those who read Chinese, but it gave me this pleasant, unusual feeling of there being a part of the story that exists for itself and isn't for me. It's hard to put into words, but it was a really nice feeling.

Novel: *In Other Lands*, by Sarah Rees Brennan. It's hilarious and touching, and I fell in love with it immediately. The author describes it as the story of the grouchiest kid in fantasyland, which was already enough to hook me, honestly, but then it goes on to be sweet and honest and funny and... yeah. Plus it's got an openly bisexual protagonist and a strong focus on friendship as the emotional core of the book, plus it overtly pulls into question a lot of tired and sometimes problematic fantasy tropes... It's just so good. I hugged the book when I finished reading it.

Lastly, what's on the horizon for you? Tell us about any forthcoming publications, works in progress, or anything else you'd like to mention.

I've got one super top secret thing that's very exciting but that I unfortunately can't talk about – let's just say my experience in constructing languages has come into play for a really cool project that will be announced sometime in 2018! Apart from that, I have an ongoing linguistics educational video channel on YouTube that I do with my friend Moti Lieberman called *The Ling Space*, we've been going for about three years and it's pretty great. And I'm hoping to finish my second round of revisions on a novel manuscript by the end of the year!

Phaser

Cameron Van Sant

Mom asked, point blank: "Are you doing *things* with that girl?"

"That girl" was named Rose, and the *Donnie Darko* DVD Elizabeth and Mom were watching was a loan from her. Elizabeth had planned to watch Rose's favorite movie intently, but instead she found herself hugging a throw pillow, giggling, and rambling about Rose-said-this and Rose-did-that.

Elizabeth itched her head, and the truth slipped out before she could catch it: "She's my girlfriend." Might as well tell her everything. "I'm a lesbian."

Mom stopped the DVD, but didn't look away from the screen.

"No, you're not."

"Yes, I am! We're—"

"You spend too much time with her and you're confused. It's a phase."

Elizabeth stood up, hands curled in fists by her sides. "I was born this way," she said.

Mom laughed, not amused but incredulous, and angry. "What?" Her tone deepened: *"What?* You were not."

"I was and there's nothing you can do about it!"

Mom looked at her finally, eyes tired but steely. "I can ground you."

Mom turned on all of the lights and marched to Elizabeth's room, mumbling "I've had enough!" She collected Elizabeth's laptop and her iPod, and ripped down the posters of Beyoncé, Jessie J, *Pretty Little Liars* and *Glee*. She piled up the contraband, and stuffed inside it was a photo of Rose—brown-skinned raven-haired girl holding a fat tabby, and smiling her blue braces grin.

Mom stashed the pile behind her own bedroom door. "You'll go to school, you'll come straight home, and you'll go nowhere else."

"I still have to go to rehearsal!" Elizabeth played the pirate Dick Johnson in the community theater production of *Treasure Island*. "That's my future!"

"Don't make me say it twice," Mom said. "Get to your room!" Elizabeth obeyed, and slammed her door shut.

She threw on a knee-length unisex t-shirt, wrapped herself up in a comforter cocoon, and cried in bed. She plugged her earbuds into her phone, which somehow escaped the contraband pile, and through them, Tegan and Sara sang, "Good-bye, Good-bye" on loop.

She texted Rose again: "I know you're asleep, but if you see this, text back, babe." She sent her eight texts and called her twice. Rose didn't reply or pick up. But if she would, Elizabeth knew, it would soothe her sobbing chest, smooth away her smothering long hair, and clear her head, buzzing with so much adrenaline it felt like she was floating.

She *was* floating.

Elizabeth poked her head out of the blanket. A hazy pink light surrounded her. She looked down—her bed was several feet away. She slapped her blanket against her sides with her elbows before it could fall and then she saw she was floating straight at the ceiling. She screamed, but her body gently phased outside—when she looked down, she saw her roof, receding into the night. Tegan and Sara chirped, "Good-bye, good-bye, like the first time."

Elizabeth looked for the source of the pink light, and above her hovered a giant silver spaceship. She fumbled for her phone's camera app but she phased inside before she could open it.

Blobby beings with colorful glistening skin, long tube arms, and no faces walked around a room with buttons and gadgets on the walls. Some stretched up, twice their original height, to touch the buttons with many waving fingers. A purple one touched her

117

blanketed shoulder. She screamed and jumped away. It spun its head in a circle, and then pointed with seven fingers. It slowly walked in that direction. She yanked out her earbuds and followed it down a series of glowing halls.

They arrived in a little circular room with a row of four stools bolted to the floor, and a ring of iridescent lights set into the wall at chest-level. Under the lights was a parallel ring of panels.

The being pulled a cord from under a panel, and snapped the end of it around her wrist. It glowed and pale blue light pulsed from the circle on her wrist, down the cord, and into the wall.

The being slithered out and closed the door, and the lights around the wall lit up the same blue as the color coming from her wrist.

Elizabeth yanked at the cord, but it wouldn't come off. She could spin the cord around her wrist, but couldn't see how it connected to itself—it formed a perfect circle.

She grabbed her phone and punched in 911. It rang and picked up. She heard a voice on the other end, but she couldn't make out what it said.

"This is gonna sound crazy," she said, "but I've been abducted by aliens!"

She heard the voice again clearly, and it wasn't speaking English.

The purple being opened the door, and Elizabeth dropped the phone back into her cocoon. It held out its many fingers toward her.

"What?" Elizabeth said.

The being said, in her voice, "This is gonna sound crazy, but I've been abducted by aliens!" It wiggled its fingers.

She unplugged the earbuds and dropped the phone in its fingers. It retracted the arm and the phone phased into its body. It closed the door.

Elizabeth smeared the wet off her face with her palm and sat on a stool at the end of the row. Her brain scrambled to come up with an explanation—was this an elaborate prank by her mom to "scare her straight"? Was her mom secretly an alien? She crumpled the earbud cords. That made no sense, but she didn't know how any of this could be real.

The door opened, and a 20-something strode in, hair dyed pink, half-shaved, the other half hanging in a page boy cut. The stranger wore a black tank top and purple boxers. They had the same face as Elizabeth.

"I remember this," the stranger said.

"I don't remember you," Elizabeth said. "Are we cousins?"

"No," the stranger smiled. They climbed over the stools, and eyed the panels on the back wall. "I saw me get it from… this one!" They opened a panel, pulled out another cord, and slapped it around their own wrist. Green light pulsed from their arm, and traveled down the cord into the wall. The blue wall lights diluted green until they settled on an aquamarine color.

"What year is it?" the stranger asked Elizabeth.

She wondered why that would be a relevant question. Had this person been trapped here for years?

"2013."

The person grinned. "I'm you, in 2018."

Eyes wide, Elizabeth looked the person up and down. "Time travel exists?!"

The person put their hand out. "I'm Z, you at age 21."

"Maybe we shouldn't touch. What if the universe explodes?"

"It won't. Trust me, I used to be you. I saw this whole night, as you, when I was 16. We had this exact conversation, and then shook hands. It was fine."

Elizabeth looked down at the hand, just like hers, only with black nails. They shook. Nothing exploded.

"Then what happened with the aliens?"

Z sat on the stool next to Elizabeth. "Don't worry about them. We get kidnapped, the lights around here flash, they drop you off unharmed at your time in a few hours."

"What about the lights coming out our arms? Are they like... siphoning off our energy?" Like a Sailor Moon villain, she thought, but did not say.

"Maybe? I don't know," Z laughed. "But I felt okay afterwards. It's fine. Whatever they're taking doesn't hurt us at all."

Elizabeth fiddled with the earbud cords. "Do I get my phone back?"

Z squinched their eyes up. "I don't remember that part."

"Well, start telling me what you do remember! Tell me about Rose, and Mom, and theater!"

"Something more important first: I'm not a girl."

"What?" Elizabeth frowned. "I thought you were me."

The lights glimmered greener.

"I am you. I'm also something called genderqueer. Google that when you get home."

"Mom took my laptop."

"Oh!" Z's eyes widened. "This is the night you came out the first time!"

"Wait, the first time?"

121

"Look, the quick version is I'm not really a woman. Or a man either. I have a whole 'nother gender. To me, it's something between 'man' and 'woman'." They looked up, smiling. "It's a masculine gender, but with some androgynous and feminine attributes too."

"Wait, does something happen to our..." Elizabeth glanced down at Z's boxers.

Z laughed. "It's not about genitals. Your gender is in here." They tapped their head. "Think about it: You've never really been into girly stuff. When you were little, and you played with Kevin and Michael Espinoza and their friends, you were a total tomboy."

Elizabeth thought about playing Yu-Gi-Oh cards with Kevin and Michael, how they periodically picked on her as it amused them and she'd run home crying. She wasn't sure about Z's version of the story, but she remembered when she was a kid she wished she was a real tomboy. She didn't think she'd been cool enough to use the label. But something about this whole speech excited her.

"When you grew up," Z went on, "and hit puberty, and the guys stopped playing with you and Mom bought you girly clothes, you got girly, just because you thought you had to."

Elizabeth didn't like thinking about puberty at all. It was gross, all the stupid pink products and the condescending health teacher voices.

"You're not a girl," Z said. "You're something else. You'll meet radical queers when you go to college; they'll clear up a lot."

"Yeah okay, I'll have to think about that," Elizabeth said, itching her scalp. "But are you still a lesbian?"

"You have to be a girl to be a lesbian. And stop itching! That's a gross habit, no one likes watching you do that."

Elizabeth put her hands behind her back and flicked at the stuff under her nails. "But you still only like girls, right?"

Z shrugged.

"Don't tell me you like guys! You can't! I just told Mom I was a born lesbian, and she called it a phase!"

The lights flashed blue before fading back to aquamarine.

"Calm down," Z said. "I don't date guys. I date other non-binary people and women."

Elizabeth stared down at the shiny stools, and then she looked up, eyes wide. Rose. "You're not with Rose anymore."

"Yeah," Z said, itching their shaved head half, then suddenly stopped and looked at their hand. "That… ended."

Elizabeth grabbed Z's shoulder. "Why? What happened? Did she leave us?"

"I don't know if I should talk about this part," Z said. "Rose is so important to you, and…" Their eyes shifted away. "I don't want you to, you know, ruin it based on the future."

"I won't ruin it! I'll change the future!"

"Listen, I ruined it based on what future-me said. I did something terrible just because I knew it wouldn't last. Oh, hell, I've already told you it wouldn't last."

"I'll learn from your mistake and do something different!"

Z pursed their lips in a pout. "I said the exact same thing." They rolled their eyes to the side. "And then, future-me said that. And that."

Before Elizabeth could press them more, the door opened, and a man strode in. He wore sweat pants and a t-shirt, and had black stubble all up his face and down his neck. Elizabeth wasn't sure if he was her age or 30-something; he had little eye wrinkles and a sharp widow's peak, but he had a baby face. He also looked like a relative.

He scowled at the two of them, and sat on the far seat. He rested his face in his hands. "I have a presentation tomorrow morning. I don't have time for this nonsense."

"Who is this?" Elizabeth whispered to Z.

"This room is tiny and I can hear you!" he snapped. "Who do you think it is? Don't you remember from last time?"

"His name is Dennis," Z said to Elizabeth. They turned to him. "It's their first time. Don't *you* remember when you were them?"

"It's been a while," he grumbled, itching his shaved hair.

"Stop doing that!" Z said.

"You clearly can't stop!" Dennis said.

"Wait," Elizabeth said. "You're another future self?"

"I'm you in 2029, at 32 years old."

Elizabeth looked him over, in awe. He had an Adam's apple, a deep voice, and his face was different somehow—more angular. He looked the same height as her, but his bare arms had lean muscles that made him seem bigger.

Z held up their wrist. "Go find your cord."

"Why should I?" he said. "What do these aliens ever do for us?"

"I remember where it was," Z said, and they got up and opened a panel by Dennis' head. They snapped the cord around his arm. Red light pulsed around his wrist and into the wall. The color mix on the wall dulled to a murky red-brown.

Dennis seemed upset about something. Elizabeth asked, "Do the aliens do something terrible?"

He gave her the same steely and tired look Mom gave her earlier, and he said, "Imagine you meet here with yourself at, I don't know, six and ten. Six-year-old you needs his hand held, and ten-year-old you thinks he knows it all." The light on the wall became redder. "Both of the early yous are working on things you figured out years ago, like manners and multiplication. Imagine you're forced to look at what an embarrassing snot-nosed kid you used to be. Then you'll know how I feel."

Z looked at Elizabeth through lidded eyes. "He was an asshole last time too."

"I'm just tired, okay! The aliens didn't exactly call ahead and work around my schedule."

"That's not an excuse." Z flipped their page boy hair to the other side of their head. The wall light got murky again. "This meeting is an important, rare event."

Dennis looked around the room. "Maybe I'll lay on the floor. God, this lighting is annoying as hell."

Z sighed and propped their face in their hand. "How's it going with… what's his name? Chang?"

Dennis glared at them. "His name is Chengen, and we're doing fine. Pay attention to his name when you meet him. We have an anniversary coming up, and we're very happy."

"Wait, what?" Elizabeth stood, and her blanket fell, and she caught it and yanked it up around her shoulders, and then she dropped the earbuds. "You're dating a man?" She scrambled on the floor for the headphones. "You can't—I just told Mom—"

"That you're born a lesbian, yeah," Dennis said, and the lights became redder again. "In case you haven't noticed, it's not true."

"You can't do that!" Elizabeth shook her fist with her headphones in it. "Mom said it was just a phase, and you'll prove her right!"

"Why is that my fault?" he snapped, loud. He looked alert now. "Unlike you, I'm in a happy, fulfilling relationship, and I'm more at ease with myself and my body than I've ever been—than *you've* ever been. Being authentically myself is more important than proving Mom wrong. You won't be a teenager forever."

"But if I don't like men, how can you?" Elizabeth said, plopping back down on her stool.

Dennis ignored her question. "If you want to blame someone for undoing your coming out, then blame him." He nodded at Z.

"Like you didn't do the same exact thing," Z snapped.

"What?" Elizabeth said.

Z itched their head. "Dammit." They clasped their knees. "Can't be a lesbian if you're not a girl. I told Mom we're genderqueer."

"She'd say you made it up!" Elizabeth said.

"Oh, she did. Later, I thought I was genderfluid, like sometimes I had a male gender and sometimes I had a female gender, and I told her that."

"She's not gonna listen to you! She'll say it's a phase for sure!"

"She did, but being honest felt more important," Z said, squinting. Dennis snorted. "Then, I realized I'm properly genderqueer, like I thought before, so I told her that."

"In case you're wondering," Dennis said, "She didn't try to do right by him during any of this. Didn't call him 'them' or 'they.' Just kept saying 'she' and 'daughter' and said, 'When are you gonna date a nice boy?' Being non-binary fucking sucks. Barely anyone gendered him right; even some of his college girlfriends called him 'she,' and felt perfectly fine calling themselves lesbians. Do you remember that time at the—"

"At the Denny's—" Z chimed in.

"And he refused to tip that waiter until he called him something other than 'ma'am.'"

"Anything else, I said. I was on my second date with Georgia Roussos, and I'd had enough alcohol to convince myself arguing made me look cool, though I was really just sick of getting misgendered."

Elizabeth pulled the blanket tighter around her shoulders. "But what happened to Rose?"

"Of all our disappointing news about the future, you have to let that one go," Dennis said. "She's your first girlfriend, for god's sake. You know better than to expect to be with her forever."

Elizabeth looked from Z to Dennis. "What else should I be disappointed about?"

Dennis sighed, and looked over at the lights closest to him. "Did I mention where I work?"

"You will soon," Z said.

Dennis crossed his legs and arms. "I work at an office," he said. "We do insurance for construction workers."

Z clucked and shook their head at him. Elizabeth stared at him, eyes wide. "But you're still trying to act, right?"

"*I'm* in the college theater department," Z jumped in. "I'm getting an acting degree. I'm Viola in our production of *Twelfth Night*. I'm—*We're*—doing great. Don't listen to this long-ass discouraging speech he's about to give."

"Before you can be an actor," Dennis clasped his hands together, "you have to eat, and in order to do that, you need a day job. The kind of jobs willing to employ *this*," he gestured up and down Z, "don't pay a living wage. If I wanted to eat something other than Top Ramen every night, I needed a proper office job. The professional world did not give a fuck about genderqueer identity, and my options were A: dress like a femme woman again, or B: be a man."

Now the lights were solid red. "One of those options seemed like hell, the other seemed intriguing. So before I aged out of Mom's insurance," he gestured up and down his body, "I transitioned. I went on hormones, got a couple surgeries, and as time went by, the more I thought, 'Why didn't I do this years ago?'" He didn't seem tired at all now, and rambled on, animated. "No one called me 'miss' or 'ma'am' or 'she,' people started treating me with a little respect, and guys stopped harassing me on the street. Besides bisexuals, I could date straight women and gay guys, and I started to feel at home in this old body of ours."

"Some of that's just male privilege," Z said, and the lights glimmered brown for a moment.

Dennis took a slow, deep breath, and looked at Elizabeth. "The reason you are so hell-bent on staying with Rose, and Mom thinking we're a lesbian, has nothing to do with love. It's because Rose is the femme one; contrasted with her, you come across a little bit masculine. You love that. It's a validation you never felt before, but you know for sure if you dated a straight guy, it would vanish like that." He snapped his fingers. "All your drama," then he turned to indicate Z with his chin, "and all your transitions are all about feeling masculine. You two are slowly unearthing the fact that we have been a boy, a *man*, this whole time. I am the end goal."

Elizabeth itched her scalp, staring at the lights in middle distance. She wondered if she really was a man. She didn't think of herself as butch. But she had wanted to cut her hair for a while. She touched her long hair.

She remembered one time Rose put her arm around her shoulders, and Elizabeth wanted to move it so her arm could be the one on Rose's shoulders, but didn't know why, and she didn't do it because she didn't want to act weird.

"While you were misgendering me you forgot to explain why you ditched acting," Z said.

Dennis scowled at them. "I'm getting there. I got my corporate job; I got some money; I got a gym membership and nice clothes and drove down to L.A. every few days and auditioned. All that, only to find out there aren't any roles for a trans man. Not in 2025, which was the last time I went to an audition. If a movie or show wants a trans man, they want exactly one, and they call up Tom Phelan or Brian Michael Smith or Jack Wayans. Or a cis woman."

"Who's Jack Wayans?" Z asked.

"You'll know. When he comes out, it'll be big," he dismissed them with a wave. "I tried auditioning for roles assumed for cis men, but with these hips and this baby face and the fact that I'm shorter than your average actress in heels meant I fell, well, short of the male ideal. I was getting older and looking weirder and I wasn't getting roles. Community theater seemed like a consolation prize."

He leaned against the wall. "I threw myself into work at the office, and now I'm doing great. I advanced to a manager position, fourteen employees report to me, and I'm really proud of my accomplishments."

"You don't sound proud," Z said.

The red lights dropped to the murky brown color again.

"Don't talk to me like that," he snapped. "I have to be happy or people will say, 'He transitioned for no reason.'"

"You mean you weren't born that way," Elizabeth said.

"Fuck you," he said.

There was a knock on the door, and the three looked at it. It creaked and opened slowly.

"Hello, all. I'm now agender, ey/em pronouns, if you please."

The person who appeared had the same aged baby face that Dennis had, but now wrinkled. Eir face was clean shaven, and ey'd grown eir hair into a coifed faux-hawk. Ey wore a closely fitted jacket that flared at the hips, dress pants, and black boots with platform heels. Ey swiped off eir glittery sunglasses, arm trailing in an arc.

"I'm Zabeth," ey smiled. "The year is 2062, I am all of you at 65 years old."

The other three stared. "That gets me every time," Dennis said.

"How come the oldest of us is the most fabulous?" Z asked.

Zabeth put eir sunglasses on eir head and sat on the empty stool between Z and Dennis.

"He said…" Elizabeth stood, pointing at Dennis and her blanket finally fell to the ground. "He said he was the end goal!" The lights flashed aquamarine for a second.

"That's what made the most sense to me at the time," Zabeth said. "But like I said, since then I decided not to have a gender."

"You can't just decide," Dennis said.

"You did," Z said.

Amidst the banter, the lights flashed from one color to another.

Elizabeth sat down in a huff, blanket discarded at her feet. "Does that mean we came out to Mom as a weird identity *again*?"

"Yes," Zabeth said, voice soft. Ey held eir hand to Elizabeth. She awkwardly put her hand in eirs. It was soft with wrinkles, and the wall lights became as pure blue as the light coming from Elizabeth's hand. "I appreciate that you started your path by being honest with Mom and involving her in your journey. You didn't have to, and because you did, she punishes you for selfish reasons. I just want you to know, in the long run it'll strengthen your relationship."

"When?" Dennis snorted. "We're not talking."

Zabeth let go of Elizabeth's hand and took Z's. The wall light became green. "I appreciate you for transitioning time and time again, being true to yourself despite the fact that barely anyone recognizes that self." Z smiled and shrugged mock-modestly.

"And you," ey turned to Dennis. He crossed his arms, pre-emptively cutting off the hand-holding. Ey put eir hand on his shoulder, and the wall lights became red. "I appreciate you for taking a leap of faith—starting hormones and having surgeries. Even though I have no gender, I needed a specific body, and that's the one you got us."

Dennis made a "hrmph" sound of acknowledgment.

Zabeth stood up, and the light color became murky again. "I'm not going to say much more."

"Just tell me one thing," Dennis said. "Is—is Chengen fucking around?"

"You already know the answer to this question," Zabeth said.

"You said your relationship was happy!" Elizabeth said.

Dennis sniffled and looked at the wall. Zabeth walked behind the row of stools and touched another panel on the wall. Out popped a metal case, displaying glittering pie charts and bar graphs. Ey put eir sunglasses on, looked it over, then whipped them off again and said, "It's time to go home."

Ey flipped a dial on the case, and the cords detached from everyone's hands and zipped into their respective wall panels. Ey opened the door and led the other three through the halls. The beings they passed glowed, squished down short, and waved their little fingers at Zabeth.

Back in the big room with all the buttons, the three younger people gathered together, eyeing the aliens. Zabeth put the case on the ground, and the aliens gathered around it, touching it with their little fingers. One plucked it from the others, and plugged a hose into it. The case vibrated, and the ceiling showered everyone in purple mist. The aliens held their fingers up to the mist and spun, making cooing noises.

Dennis began to glow pink. "I am the end game," he said to Zabeth. "I know who we are. I'll change the future and I won't become you."

"We'll see," Zabeth smiled and waved. He vanished.

Z glowed pink next. "It didn't feel as much like a rerun as I thought. Can't wait to see you all again," and they vanished.

Elizabeth noticed her hands glowed pink. She grabbed Zabeth's arm. "Do you become an actor? What about Rose? What was I born to be?"

Zabeth shook eir head. A rectangle phased out of eir palm, and ey put it in Elizabeth's hand. It was her phone. "No one asks about the damn aliens."

And then Elizabeth was falling in the sky.

Author Interview: Cameron Van Sant

Cameron Van Sant is a writer and educator who lives in California. I asked him some questions about writing, gender, and his cat Wachowski.

Could you start by telling me where you got the idea for "Phaser" from?

Before I start, I'd just like to say that I will refer to the main character from Phaser with "they" pronouns to answer your questions. Not to say that those are the character's "correct" or "true" pronouns. Since the character is "unhinged from time" in the context of the story, I don't think they have "true" pronouns the way that most trans people do.

To answer your question, I have to give some background information on my coming out story: Trans people who come out are expected to legitimize their identity by saying they were "born that way" and prove it by listing gender-non-conforming behavior they exhibited since time immemorial. That narrative was a large obstacle for me to realize my true gender.

Boy Cameron never thought of himself as a boy, much less said anything about it. Though I could make a list of stereotypically boyish behaviors or interests I had as a kid, I could just as easily make a list of stereotypically girlish behaviors or interests that would "contradict" my other list.

I was an adult when I first started to suspect that I was male. I had serious doubts because I didn't have that "born this way" evidence that I saw so many trans people had. Lots of trans people are compelled to go into therapy in order to get access to trans healthcare, but I went willingly because I really needed help figuring out my gender.

As an exercise, my therapist assigned me to write a letter to myself when I was young. Writing that letter forced me to face the truth—Boy Cameron would be ecstatic to meet me because being male is my most authentic self. Because of that, I very much wanted the sci-fi part of the letter to be real; I wanted to send my letter to Boy Cameron and tell him who he really was and that things would be okay. The impact that would have had on my past self and the heartache it would have prevented would be enormous.

That exercise was the seed for this story. Now that I think about it, even though the main character and I check several different identity boxes and our transition stories differ, in a way, I'm pretty sure this story is a kind of fantasy for me.

I think authors are often wary of depicting gender fluidity in the way you have because the idea of gender being fluid or changeable is often used against trans people (eg "you'll change your mind later" or "it's all a phase"). How did you navigate representing this aspect of many people's experience of gender without reinforcing those ideas?

I am going to take this question as a compliment, because I'm not sure if I successfully avoided reinforcing negative ideas, ha ha.

When pressured to accommodate the "born this way" defense, out trans people are pressured to resist further gender experimentation or to suppress a gender that might evolve or fluctuate. All trans people have our gender interrogated, and losing access to a defense cis people easily understand can be terrifying.

However, I think that many trans people, like the main character in "Phaser", come out multiple times. Sometimes genders change; sometimes you don't have enough information to realize your correct gender the first time. Just because you came out multiple times doesn't mean your genders weren't and aren't biologically real.

In "Phaser", I tried to portray a gender evolution that had to occur in order for the character to be their most authentic self. I tried to show why the main character had to be Elizabeth before they could one day be Zabeth. I wanted the narrative to show that it's okay that main character did not come out "right" the first time, and it's okay that they experimented with their gender and made mistakes.

Shout out: Tyler Ford and Sassafras Lowry have each written great essays about their different coming outs/presentations that are essential for anyone who wants to explore this topic further.

Were there any other works that influenced this story? Are there other works of fiction you've enjoyed reading (or watching) that explore diverse gender identities?

I watched a lot of *Doctor Who* in college. Now that I think about it, I can see traces of *Doctor Who* in "Phaser", especially how humans' personal lives have the potential to matter to time-traveling aliens.

As far as books with diverse gender identities, I read both *Ninefox Gambit* and *Raven Stratagem* by Yoon

Ha Lee, and they've been some of my favorite books of the year. *Raven Stratagem* has upped the level of queerness and gender complexity since *Ninefox Gambit*, and there are three trans-ish characters. One character is trans in the traditional way, and two others are gender complex in a way only possible through sci-fi, and I enjoy the contrast.

If you could go to any real place in the world, and any fictional place, where would you go?

I would love to go to Iceland. I'm not sure why Iceland looms large in my imagination, but I'm somewhat charmed by their Viking history, adorable horses, and love of books. Oh yeah, and their progressive LGBTQ policies.

For the fictional place, I think I'd like to go to the San Francisco of Malinda Lo's *Inheritance*, which is the docking place for a spaceship of cool polyamorous non-binary mostly-friendly aliens.

Tell me a story about your cat please! (And if you could satisfy my curiosity... how do you know they're agender?)

Once, while playing Ellen DeGeneres' Heads Up game, I was trying to get my enbyfriend, Em, to guess the clue "Howling". I was tired, sprawled in bed, and only made a warbly howl sound. Our cat, Wachowski, immediately jumped on the bed, stood on my arm, and started sniffing my face. When they were satisfied I had not turned into some other type of animal, they turned around and hopped off the bed. The part that amuses me the most is that my poor imitation of a howl would be clearly perceived as human to pretty much anyone else, but Chow needed to make sure.

Em and I are both trans and both love cats. As a new couple, we joked that one day we would adopt a genderqueer cat. When Wachowski chose us (they cutely walked-while-stretching in our direction at the shelter; it was impossible to say no) we decided that we would officially designate Chow a genderqueer cat and they-pronoun them. Sometime later, we decided that Chow was agender, in the sense that they do not have a human gender.

We're half-joking and half-serious with their gender. We do they-pronoun Chow and correct most people who use other pronouns (Vets get a pass). It seems more correct to me to use neutral pronouns for Chow rather than assign a human gender based on their genitals. Most importantly: Chow cares about treats, not human words. They're chill with the pronouns.

Can you recommend a short story and a novel to readers?

Right now I'm reading an older collection of Native American women's short stories called *Spider Woman's Granddaughters* edited by Paula Gunn Allen. There's a short story in it I love called "Warriors" by Anna Lee Walters about two Pawnee girls who are intrigued by a homeless camp near their house. This whole anthology is very good so far—it's challenged the way I think about short fiction and what types of narratives I, as a white person, find valuable.

One of my favorite books of all time is *The Drowning Girl* by Caitlín R. Kiernan. It's a dark novel about a queer painter named Imp who has schizophrenia. The two women most important to her are her off-and-on girlfriend, Abalyn (video game reviewer, trans, definitely real) and a mysterious woman named Eva Canning (painter, not trans, possibly not real). Through an exploration of history, myth, art, and her relationships, Imp struggles to maintain her mental health and learn exactly who is Eva Canning. The book is great overall—I can't speak to the portrayal of schizophrenia, but the trans portrayal is great.

Lastly, what's on the horizon for you? Tell us about any forthcoming publications, works in progress, or anything else you'd like to mention.

I have another short story coming out in January 2018—it's called "The Mermaid and the Pirate" and it's going to be published in an anthology called *Queerly Loving Volume Two*. "The Mermaid and the Pirate" is about a butch space pirate named Jean who begins a flirtation with a butch mermaid the pirates found swimming through space. It's a rollicking little romantic space adventure, and I hope you'll like it.

Other than that, I am writing more LGBTQ science fiction and fantasy short stories that I hope will reach the public soon!

Grow Green

Rem Wigmore

Nederene gently turned the bell of one flower with clawed and nimble hands, inspecting how it hung heavy from the stalk. "Interesting work, Jeb. What are they for?"

Jeb sniffed a flower, tenderly. A faint spicy, floral scent drifted to eir nose, against the musty background smell of soil. The flowers smelt a little like jasmine, though they were not jasmine. Ey almost fancied ey could hear the small creatures shifting below the surface soil, worms and beetles curled up sleeping.

"Well, they're here to be lovely," Jeb said. Ey turned over another bloom carefully, looking for insect damage. "Same as any flower."

Nederene huffed, and dropped down on preer haunches. The faery had an elegant way about prin, those stark and dramatic eyes and legs with rather more joints than any human Jeb knew. But pry could still feel like a petulant child. "You know that is not what I meant! Do not 'mess'. What magic have you put in them!"

Jeb thought ey felt a tingle coming from the flower where ey touched it, coursing up eir arm. Ey withdrew eir hand. "I'm still not convinced I do that," ey said, stalling. Then: "I don't know. We'll know once they've grown, I suppose."

"Waiting for things to grow…" Nederene tilted preer head. "Silly use of time really, when you small ones get so little of it."

Jeb stood up, brushing soil off eir knees. Smudges of brown stayed on the green corduroy. Every item of clothing Jeb owned was green, except the ones that were brown. "It's not like I plan to set up camp here until they're done," ey said amused. "Watched pot never boils."

"Untrue," Nederene said, pointing one long finger at em. "One of your language-lies." Pry looked delighted.

"Yes," Jeb said, sighing out. The air here was pleasant, crisp and stirring in eir lungs. "You found it."

Whatever charm they bore, the flowers were nearly grown. Jeb realised with a start that slow as the seasons seemed to turn, spring would soon be over, and summer here. Nederene wouldn't be a pry any more. Ey didn't know if pry wanted em to use the same words as last year or a different set, though pry had been consistent so far: O, ors, orself was probably Jeb's favourite of preers, but autumn was a while off. Ey would have to ask prin.

It was odd, being friends with one of the fae. Pronoun sets were the least of it, of course; Jeb even had human friends who rotated theirs, though not with the seasons, not as spring bloomed into summer mellowed into autumn crept slowly into winter's sleep. This thing, the plants Jeb grew having odd properties and growing too fast, that had never happened before ey met Nederene. No one else seemed able to find the garden, either.

"I hope you will stay alive long enough for them to grow," Nederene said, swinging graceful into step. Pry gave em a look that ey interpreted roughly as anxious. "Oh so little time."

"I should have at least another twenty years, touch wood."

Nederene's shoulders bunched up around preer ears. "There isn't any," pry said, sort of hollow and anxious.

"Language-lies, sorry. Sorry. I'm sure I should be fine." Ey should be, yes. Jeb sighed. Looked up to find eir friend surveying em with bright birdlike eyes, fretful, as though expecting Jeb to die of plague on the spot. Jeb shook eir head. "The flowers aren't ready, but here, I still have a gift for you." Ey plucked a leaf from a bush that wouldn't miss it, and reached up. Nederene hunkered down, and Jeb tucked the leaf behind the faery's ear. "There you are. Now you'll be very dashing for all the other fae ladies and gentlemen and others."

"I already have partners for the next *five* dances," pry said, glancing at Jeb out of one eye as though expecting em to be impressed. Jeb nodded solemnly. Nederene stood up straight and trilled. "And what of you! You told me last time that you met someone, have you ..." Pry winked. "Met them again?"

Jeb let out a soft huff of laughter. Then shook eir head.

"Oh," Nederene said, and patted eir shoulder. "Apologies if this saddens you."

"No, no. We did meet again. She ... didn't feel the same way, but that was fine," Jeb said, lifting eir hands in defence of an allegation Nederene hadn't made. "That was fine, of course, and we ended up ... quite good friends. I think we're good friends."

Nederene rasped preer fingers together, a noise that put Jeb in mind of crickets chirping. Jeb shrugged.

"She isn't doing well," ey said to the unasked question.

Nederene let out a soft keen, further back in the throat than any human sound. Pry loped over the gardenbed and bowed preer head, pushed it forward so their heads were pressed together. After a moment pry lifted preer arms, awkwardness in more than just the offering of the gesture but the shape of it, ungainly as a stork.

Jeb had been prideful at one point in eir life, but all ey could think about was Eun's face, the pallor in it, how odd she looked with her head shaved bare. Ey leaned silently into the embrace.

Nederene was colder than a human, and felt vaguely sharp. All the comparisons that came to Jeb's mind were faintly insulting: a jangle of trowels, origami made of spun wire. Ey let out a short unfamiliar laugh, and then closed eir mouth on the sobs that wanted to follow it.

"There there there," Nederene said softly, halfway to sing-song. Preer voice was soothing, the wind through leaves. "There there there there."

Jeb squeezed eir friend tightly, all the unfamiliar shapes, and the familiar intent. After a while, feeling calmer, ey opened eir eyes. "You're very thin, you know."

Nederene pulled back with a screech of a laugh. "With all my kind it is such! At least in this century."

Well, alright then. "You know, I used to want to be like you," Jeb said with a wave at Nederene's bone-razor thinness. "Once." Ey felt drifting, strange, a good time to take sanctuary in what ey knew was true. "Lately, sometimes, I want to be bigger. Like a mountain, like a tree. Like an old stone covered in moss. A bulwark for my friends to be safe in."

Ey closed eir eyes again. Things felt safer this way. This garden, with its walls of trees, could be anywhere, then. Could be some other world. If fairies were real why couldn't there be some other world? Where Jeb was happy and Eun was safe.

Nederene's voice seemed thin with distance when pry spoke. "I think you're that already," pry said. Then, "Are you alright?"

Here. Here, with a moth buzzing somewhere unseen in the undergrowth, the air just starting to get cold enough to bite. Ey was here. Jeb opened eir eyes, hesitated. "No. Not really."

Nederene stretched out. "I am here," pry said.

"Yes."

There was nothing else to be done today. The weeds had been plucked, the wrong insects discouraged and the right ones safeguarded. More scraps placed on the compost, and the flowers coming along well, but not grown yet. There seemed no reason to linger, though ey wanted to; wanted to with the slow torpor that came of not wanting to do anything else.

Jeb started walking, taking the path that would lead em home. The trick was not to think too hard on it, to think of other things, but Jeb didn't want to think at all right now. Ey focused on the immediate path, the crunch of shells.

Nederene stalked beside em, a silent presence. When they'd first met, even for the first several months afterwards, Jeb had found prin quite frightening.

Nothing for a while but the crunch, crunch of shells, and the soft barely audible whisper Nederene made when moving. "Maybe they will heal, this batch," pry said tentatively. "Maybe your friend will be all-manner-of-well, after a tilt of flower juices."

"Maybe." Unlikely.

A few steps more, Jeb's conscience smote em, and ey added, "Thank you, my friend."

"Always. I will be here for you for at least the next fifty years."

Something in that was almost soothing. Sometimes Nederene was childish and felt young as a flower barely into blooming, like fresh new shoots. Or in the winter like a mad and merry thing, cracking ice and flexing fingers. Sometimes pry felt like how it felt to stand beside an old boulder, or at the bottom of a cliff, by the trees that eight people linking hands couldn't form a circle around: the comforting, alarming feeling of being near something larger and older than yourself, a tangible ancient thing. Jeb smiled.

"Until then I'll see you in a week," ey said, lightly teasing.

"Stay alive, you and all those you love."

"Stay alive, you and all those you love," Jeb replied, formally. Nederene dipped preer head in a bow, a fond gesture for prin, and then Jeb was walking alone out of a narrow alleyway, graffiti on the corrugated iron fences showing cities, faces, cartoon characters, cars passing here and there in the street ahead.

Walking the Wall of Papered Peaces

Penny Stirling

They say that somewhere along the paper wall you can find your heart's peace.

They never say you can find it easily.

Florence must find the wall before she can search for her heart's peace. She had thought it would be easy but days of struggling to follow grown-over paths has gnawed at her resolve. Shielding her eyes from the sun, she glances back to remember why she set out. Yes, there in the distance: the glittering sea and, somewhere along it, home. She thinks of her family and worries about how her betrothed is doing. Is ze eating enough, is ze sulking at hir clients, has ze let Florence's clocks wind down? Does ze touch hir half of their engagement ring as often as Florence touches where her own once sat?

Farther and farther from home she walks and, though weeks soon hide the horizon, still she keeps looking back; she cannot stop thinking about how much she misses her house and work and friends and, most of all, more keenly with every day and every kilometre, her beloved. The doubts come in those moments of acute homesickness—what if she never finds the wall, what if she never finds her heart's peace, what if no one waits for her return—but Florence is used to collecting doubts as sure as the wall collects peaces. One more day, she thinks, because she cannot return lacking both passion and peace, because the difference between *your other half's got a lot of friends eh* and *aren't you good enough for your betrothed* will still harrow her. And just one more hill, because she can no longer see her home and she can no longer exactly remember the curve of her beloved's mouth upon hearing that it was not just *not yet*, it was *not ever*.

It is the sun and the moon who make the paper wall. Without something to anchor them to their hearts, peaces will float up to the sky. The celestials catch and give them a physical body before depositing them onto the wall. Without the gods to tend to them, who knows where the peaces would land?

Imagine not knowing where to seek your heart's peace.

Hilary has waited so many times that it did not sting when hir betrothed, with a *yes, but* and without meeting eyes, handed back her half of their engagement ring for safekeeping. As a child Hilary had waited every morning at her door for the walk to school—and outside the classroom for her detention, and for the bullies to stop inciting them both. As an adolescent ze waited for her to notice ze was flirting, for her to decide whether to try anything more than holding hands, for her to ever change her mind. And then ze watched, thinking they had finally met at the final halfway, as hir betrothed asked hir to wait and walked away seeking the wall of papered peaces. Merely because they weren't physically intimate?

Hilary had never understood hir beloved's lack of desire, true. But all the years they had been close and all the years they had been together it had never—except when she'd insisted they try and her adamance turned to inexplicable anguish every time—troubled hir that hir beloved did not enjoy sharing a bed. Why would it matter now? Was suddenly their house any less theirs, their relationship any less strong, their struggles and feelings any less real? What did it matter if Hilary sated hir lust with others' bodies, if other people whispered and lectured? *They* would not share in this marriage. Wasn't the ring sign enough that ze saw her as ideal? Wasn't hir proposal for vows enough? If it mattered to Hilary, wouldn't ze have left by now, found a partner better at remembering chores and anniversaries and work-life balance while ze was at it?

How long must ze wait this time?

Florence decides just one more hill and once she crests the rise, with a gasp, she sees it: a wall of paper, cacophony in colour form, extending horizon to horizon along a plateau.

Finally, here, she will find her peace. Oh, to resent her beloved's desires and mercy no longer, to be at peace enough that family scrutiny and town criticism would desolate no more. Imagine, to once again anticipate marriage with a heart of love, to adore and invigorate anew, to be enriched and reliable again. Here Florence will find a future for her relationship, somewhere along this wall.

Peaces placed on the wall are sheathed inside an origami animal, though the paper is no true replacement for their hearts. The sun uses plain paper, often bright; the moon favours patterned sheets. The origami fauna are set down haphazardly along the wall's length, its height varying greatly, and they have been deposited for years so countless that the wall verges on endless.

Pity the peaces whose animals have become their coffins.

Hilary will wait no more. Damn anyone who thinks their marriage cannot succeed, anyone who put this fool notion in hir beloved's head. Damn having to wind the clocks, damn returning from morning surf to empty house, ignoring when people ask what's happened, buying fresh goat's milk in case hir beloved returned that day, seeing their pinboard of wedding ideas, automatically making two cups of tea, listening to breaking waves in the evening and wondering if hir beloved heard them too, waking up from nightmares and being unable to check her safety, clutching their ring halves and thinking over and over about the last words they shared. Damn her for leaving. *Damn hir for letting her leave.*

Hastily ze prepares. Ze speaks to parent and in-laws, entrusts sister with hir half of the engagement ring along with its pair, and then ze walks away from the sea, leaving plumbing gear next to half-finished escapements. Somewhere there is a wall and somewhere along that wall hir beloved needlessly walks. Hilary does not quite know what ze will do when ze finds her, but ze will have time to practice.

Florence begins her search proper and walks along the non-metaphorical paper wall. On the first day she tried to pick up an orange swan, just to look, but the peace within the origami screamed for its true heart so loudly that it scored each of her fingers with paper cuts. There must be a peace of her very own, waiting for her, for only her. She studies the wall methodically, ensuring she looks at every single origami animal that it comprises. After coming so far, she must not miss finding her peace. There is so much she must return to; she only hopes she will return quickly. It had taken her years to notice her beloved's feelings, months to work through her thoughts and ask hir out on their first date, and then years more of acting like a couple and saying *I love you* knowing she didn't mean it quite the way ze meant it before all the love she felt fused into a new experience, an intensity of feelings she giddily realised was the *I love you* love that ze felt. She had at first assumed reciprocating hir physical feelings followed too, but when even her newfound love could not mask the revulsion that came from those acts, that particular intimacy, then there were the months that almost ruined them before they came to an agreement that Florence hadn't agreed to.

For a couple that had waited so long, surely another wait for her to find peace would be nothing.

Florence lays one hand over the other, intertwines her fingers and imagines her betrothed walks beside her.

Lifeline to some, the wall is a one-way lure for others. And to the rest of us, it is a thief.

Lost peace begets lost peace.

Florence stares at the stars. The moonlight is no longer bright enough for her to continue searching past sunset, yet more and more she seems to walk the paper wall even while asleep. It used to be that she could only find peace in her dreams; now she wakes, every morning, to tears and a fading memory of nightmares. Sometimes she finds her peace, only for the origami to crumble at her touch. Other times she becomes a heart's peace, trapped and screaming on the wall, watching someone both angry and sad walk by. She stares at the stars, too tired to look for constellations, hugging herself and wishing her beloved could soothingly comb her hair and whisper epic poetry.

Florence, though, is not sure that she deserves comfort. She'd gotten used to arguing with her beloved, but she couldn't cope with gossip and criticisms from neighbours? What kind of spouse *would* she have been able to aspire to? Neither able to *truly* grant her spouse happiness, nor able to be happy at the relief her spouse found for them both? Such fortune, to have an accommodating partner who avoided bothering her about distressing details and consensus, and yet Florence could not find peace in their seaside house full of love? What kind of spouse could she be, empty of peace, and what kind of marriage could she hope for once misery and bitterness congested her? But in trying to strengthen herself—*themselves*—she has abandoned her beloved and perhaps splintered their relationship beyond repair anyway.

Further dreams come: stealing and setting alight her beloved's peace, folding her beloved into a crane, choosing between her peace and hir life. Florence wakes clutching her nude finger and shudders, wondering how anyone could have tolerated her selfishness.

For who and what does she walk?

Hilary has little to do but walk and think. As the kilometres fall away ze wonders whether ze will find the wall and hir betrothed. Ze looks behind sometimes, trying to see the glittering sea, and thinks of the people ze misses, the jobs ze owes, the spare boots ze regrets not packing. Every time, ze pulls at the finger which should bear hir engagement ring and turns hir back on it to continue hir quest. Hir betrothed had long been hir friend, often hir hero; ze cannot give up. Yet, with nothing else to do, ze begins to recall the discussions they'd had about intimacies. Not every single one—like the noon chorus of clocks, most coalesced—but enough that ze wonders how ze could have called them anything less than arguments.

Hilary had never tried to understand why hir beloved did not enjoy or desire lovemaking. Ze had accepted it, just as ze accepted hir beloved would never wake before sunrise to watch hir surf; ze had ignored it, as if it were simply an absence of birthmarks on hir beloved's thigh; ze had unquestioningly and without seeking approval worked around it, just like when hir beloved found others to talk to about clockwork. But now ze thinks and, seeking the one who found no peace at home, ze questions hirself.

Hurt and disconcerted, Hilary blames hir beloved before ze criticises hirself. Every time ze thinks *you could have told me, you could have explained why I upset you, you could have done more* Hilary remembers *you did and I ignored you, you tried to and I trivialised it*. The only peace ze had cultivated was hir own.

Hadn't ze heard what the neighbours whispered—not about surfers, not about clockmakers—and what family insinuated, what pub locals said to their faces? Hadn't ze learned anything from their bullied school days? Hadn't ze seen hir beloved's reactions, especially after they became engaged? Hadn't ze brushed aside any doubts hir betrothed had raised about being a spouse so incomplete, just because *ze* had no doubts or cares? What else had Hilary ignored?

A long time ago, the sun and the moon each hid each other's peace amongst the mortals'. Though both have long feared that their partner will stop chasing and courting if they find their peace, they can do nothing but delay the inevitable; one day both the sun and the moon will descend to the paper wall to search for their peace of heart.

And find one another.

Hilary finds no tracks at the wall—nor a trace that hir betrothed even reached this far, either, but if ze's learned something about ignorance it's only to recognise it—for a kilometre each direction and ze stares at the damned origami pieces, knowing that if ze picks the wrong way she might never find hir betrothed.

"Honey, dearest, where are you?" ze says and waits, as if the wall would telegraph a route, and waits, as if hir heart would resonate with not a peace but a peace-mate, and waits, and chooses to walk with the sun at hir back.

Florence wonders if she has ever done anything but walk the paper wall. Sometimes she stops or stumbles, staring as some colour or contour of the wall's origami hoard triggers some moment or feeling she struggles to understand. Curl of a rack and snail, waking from fever hearing snores, giddy revelations and reciprocations of affections, parent-in-law's quilt, contentment, secrets whispered before dawn. She can, if she concentrates, picture houses by the sea, hands holding clocks, surfboards, hands passing plates, aspersions by the sea, shoulder curves, hands seeking—a heart? More hands? Half a ring?

Folded and refolded too many times, the memories are confused and faint. Will finding her heart's peace let her remember why she seeks it?

No person without a heart's peace to seek would walk the paper wall.

Not for long.

Hilary feels something is different. Ze still seeks hir betrothed, sure as night follows day and sure as the paper wall awaits hir every morning, but there is something else: a new irritation inside hir, a distracting malady that causes hir to slow and more closely examine the wall's menagerie.

Hir heart misses more than hir best friend, hir beloved, hir partner. Does ze miss peace more than ze misses hir beloved? The thoughtless peace of another's discomfort ignored; the naive peace of presumed future happiness absent self-reflection. But weren't there other peaces, too?

Hand-in-hand strolls along the beach. Eating standing up next to a bench too crowded with clock parts to permit plates. Poems and terrible jokes recited at father's grave. Head massages. Gifts—and pranks, too—left on bedside tables. Successfully shifting enough to return circulation to a limb without waking her up. Dinner and laughter with both families.

Hilary pops hir knuckles and tries to disregard the wall. Ze thinks of the future, the times of peace ze will share with hir beloved once again *only* if ze doesn't distract hirself.

Once, someone took the wrong origami animal. Instead of their own, they plucked from the wall a grey-on-black paisley dragon: the sun's peace. It did not cry and scratch; it howled and burned. Searcher bold never returned to their home and the peace profaned never returned to the wall. It fell to the ground and, over time, was torn and buried by weather and boots. When the sun hirself descends, ze will never find hir heart's peace, no matter how far along the wall ze searches.

Oh, how hir wrath will fall.

Florence... Florence walks? Florence moves? The wall moves? Wall of papers stationary. Where are the peaces' Florences? Who is the Florence—no, not Florence, Florence thinks of not Florence, who? Next to the sea, the—the sea? The—the wall of water. Wall of houses, wall of walls, wall of judgements, wall of watching hir go to—to—go to Florences? No? No, no one goes to Florence. Florence goes, to the wall. Florence cannot touch the wall, wall does not touch, except right touch for right person, will wall teach touch tolerance or will wall pass composed self-assurance, will wall provide peace before beloved's patience voids, will florence find end before beloved finds *I love you* from a paramour, before wall—be—

For—to the wall, paper wall, silent wall, walking wall, pacing wall, piecemeal wall, for?

Florence forgets to sleep sometimes, instead standing for hours, staring.

Hilary at first distrusted the recurrent wooden shrines housing jars of water with baskets of fruit, salted meat and savoury biscuits alongside more traditional luck petitions and prayer tokens—who even used this road except peace-seekers?—but hir supplies were already low from the hike and the solar eclipses etched on the shrines proved reliable.

Heavenly-bestowed lamb and peaches in hand, Hilary sits beneath an arch in the wall—less frequent than the shrines but still strange, with never a bisecting path to excuse them. Ze wonders how the gods keep its shape and whether a removed origami animal would collapse it. On the horizon storm clouds chase the sunset, dyeing the fading light red as if rage has consumed the peaces. Sheltering from rain that will never touch the wall, Hilary holds hir right hand with hir left and knows that, somewhere, hir beloved shares the absurd beauty of this wall.

Rarely does someone walk the wall of papered peaces with a companion.

Regrets are company enough.

Florence at first thinks the tugging in her chest is hunger, for she can't think when last she ate. When she stops to try and corral memories her gaze alights on a blue-and-bronze dolphin and she knows that it is her peace calling to her heart. The elation at finally finding it is short-lived, however; the dolphin is more than two metres above her reach. She turns and looks and looks, but can see nothing around to help her reach it. There have been no trees along the path for hours and the ground is too hard for her to dig up with her hands. Could she search and try to fetch something to act as a ladder? She tries to think what she's seen, tries to force a memory of passed roadside, but there is nothing but the sight of her peace—salve for heart and love—so frustratingly close. Just... *right there.*

For how long must she wait?

Hilary practices what ze will say when they meet again. They will. Ze will find hir betrothed. Ze will. They will return home and they will talk—really, *actually* talk with *listening* and decisions and agreements—and they will be happy and they will get married and be together and ze will be faithful and considerate and ze will be happy just with emotional intimacy or maybe ze will be more careful when ze visits other—*no, they will be happy*—or maybe ze will convince hir beloved that—*no, they both will be happy.* On this journey ze has ached for many things; ze knows

169

which ze misses most. Ze will remember this, the agony of needlessly losing hir beloved, and ze will remember what is most important in hir life.

Hopefully ze will. But maybe ze won't, maybe they can't be happy together—Hilary tries to accept this; ze never accepted hir father's illness and it is difficult to think hir relationship is likewise terminal—but ze'd still fight for them to *both* be happy, even separately. Ze owes hir betrothed so much. If Hilary cannot cease hir salacity and indifference, ze must at least make recompense for their damage and ensure ze cannot further distress hir beloved.

How many apologies can ze prepare?

Gold, garish, is the origami rabbit the moon finds when they descend to seek their heart's peace. They will be carrying it along the wall, uncertain despite their joy, when they find then the sun. Unable to retrieve hir own peace, the sun has taken out hir anguish on the wall; it is a backdrop of weeping ash where ze sees the moon. Eager to find blame and revenge if ze cannot find peace ze screams with a summer fire's fury that threatens to consume yet more of the wall. But the moon holds out their hand, calm even while the sun strides towards them. The paper rabbit placed on the wall so long ago sits on the moon's palm, still folded and reflecting the sun's outburst.

Graceful, glinting, is the rabbit the moon throws into the blaze when they say, "As if you'd ever let me live it down that I chose peace in the face of your pain."

Hilary carries a mauve elephant. It troubles hir. Ze wants so much to unfold it, to reunite with the peace ze'd once taken for granted, to free the soothing pulse ze feels through the paper. But hir betrothed is still out there, somewhere, and Hilary's heart burns more at the shameful thought of continuing to be so selfish. Still, the elephant stays in hand. For all hir thoughts of the partners they had been—the partners they can be again—ze cannot manage to set hir papered peace aside.

How it tempts hir.

Florence drops her pack to the ground, takes a deep breath, and then begins to climb the wall.

For how long will the screams haunt?

Will it be worth it, if you find your heart's peace on the wall? Your peace, what will it improve? When you find your home again, will your loved ones celebrate with you? The months you've missed, the work and vows you've neglected, the opportunities you've lost, the grief you've caused: how will they compare to the peace you once misplaced?

When you realise the cost of finding your peace, what will you regret?

Florence's search is concluding and her mind's wall-stupor waning now that she holds her heart's peace in a hand saturated with paper cuts. She has only to unfold the dolphin that contains it, but before she climbs back to the ground she looks down the wall. Every foot- and hand-hold has crushed the origami animals beneath. Her ascent has destroyed a whole section of peaces, rendered them unable to ever unite with their hearts. Shaking and crying, she climbs back down, for there is nothing she can do but wish and regret. Her tears follow her carnage down the wall. There are no paper-screams this time.

Hilary hears the crying first. Sounds other than the wind and birds have been rare; often ze has cupped hir ears tightly to remember the sea. Is it hir imagination or does this sound almost human? But ze hasn't seen any people since ze left home. Could it... Could it be? Ze gently tucks hir paper elephant into a breast pocket, and then Hilary runs.

Hold on.

Florence?

Florence can neither stem her tears nor tidy up the peaces she has desecrated. She knows she cannot return the wall to how it was but still she tries to reshape the origami pieces and stack them up again. Lacking the celestials' knack, they tumble back down no matter how she heaps them. Behind her on the road sits her paper dolphin, bloodied and still folded.

Florence! Florence?

Florence hears the screaming first. Sounds other than the peaces and nightmares have been rare. She turns and sees a person stumbling towards her. Unrecognisable, neither paper nor figment. And yet. Florence rubs her eyes. The sound it is making. Loud, surging, unceasing. The sea. The arguments. Images like waves: overalls and wrenches, a ring, waiting at the door, or is it two rings, a clock running fast to meet appointments just on time, no not two rings just one ring, surfacing from a wipeout, one ring in two of course, falling asleep on top unfinished clocks after agreeing not to work so late, crying and shouting and trying so much trying, one life in two people. She shudders. That is not paper. Is that peace?

"Fuck, Florence? What's wrong?"

Forward still it comes, until it stands beside Florence and reaches out its hand.

Flashes like paper spinning in the sun: hands, all to do with hands, touching gears and plates and homework and bullies' bruises, wanting to touch, not wanting to touch *there*, too much, hands, shaking, wringing, pointing, hands, begging, hands, Hilary's hands, Hilary's hands always wanting—Hilary? Hilary's hand. Here. Hilary.

Florence gasps and looks from the hand to the face. Hilary's hand. Face. Hilary. Florence begins to cry, again, and embraces her betrothed.

Maybe that's not the version of the sun and moon meeting that you've heard. They *are* gods, after all; the length of the wall is mere minutes of their lifetimes and their lives are comfortable and static. Every few decades routine nourishes a new peace, pearl-like. The moon, she rips it from her chest if she notices, just after dawn, and lets it float up. The sun is less attentive but still hir new-found peace ze always loses. Yet, each god will only have one peace hiding in the wall at a time.

Mishaps are so common.

Hilary holds hir beloved for hours. Even when they sit and catch their breaths, their arms remain entwined. At first the speech ze'd prepared turns into repeated echoes of *I'm sorry, I love you, I'm sorry* but eventually ze manages some weak semblance of it: ze hadn't really considered Florence's concerns, ze was wrong, ze shouldn't have proposed at that stage, ze's going to change, can they go back, *I love you, I'm sorry, I'm sorry.*

"How can I?" Florence points to the crushed wall section, to the peaces destroyed, and asks how she could ever open her peace after what she's done. *It's funny*, isn't it, that this all started because she didn't want to touch as much as Hilary, and now look, she's touched too much.

"Hush, hush, this isn't your fault." Hilary rests hir head on hir beloved's shoulder. "It's mine. A god may have brought your peace here, but it was I who dislodged it and it was I who waited too long. But we have each other again, and now I know peace is hard work and not to be disregarded. We can go back, can't we?"

"How can I? First I deprive you of love and now I deprive so many of peace."

Hilary thinks of their home by the sea and tries to imagine returning alone. Ze strokes the back of Florence's hand, avoiding the cut and bloodied fingers. Oh, if ze'd brought the rings. "You do not, and have *never*, deprived me of love. Love can be in the bedroom, but it is not governed by it. Love is that you always smile at me at breakfast, love is when you see my hair is down and fetch me painkillers, the way we can sit in silence together for a whole afternoon. Love is how you trust me more than any other person, trust me not to hurt you—and yet I—love is you caring. So much. And I should have spent more time caring for you. As for those... Most of them won't ever come here. Lacking peace doesn't make life unliveable, and—and besides—"

Hilary suddenly pulls away from Florence and pulls the mauve elephant out from hir pocket. "*And besides*, this is not what gives life meaning," ze says, and crushes the origami between hir hands.

Florence screams. "No, no." She pries at her beloved's hands. "No, no."

"Fine, it's fine." Hilary reveals the flattened, torn paper. "It's fine," ze says, but hir voice wavers and hir fingers twitch.

Florence gently touches the elephant, unrecognisable now. It is silent. "Why?"

"For you. Me. Us." Hilary unfolds the origami. "I drove you to this; I'm undeserving."

Florence watches her betrothed smooth the paper flat and refold it.

Fortune tellers are all Hilary knows how to make. It is not perfect, but despite the tears and the creases it works. Ze moves the quarters together and apart, smiling. "But I made another, see? There's nothing that says I can't regain peace. With you, I hope. I... If you want me to stop sleeping with others, I will. If you want me to just pick someone, I will. If you want me to shout at everyone to fuck off and that they can't see through our curtains anyway, I will. If you want me to lie to people, if you dont want to get married proper, if you... I don't know. I want to know what you want. I want to listen to what you say and what you think about what you want and what you don't want." Hilary begins to cry. "I want us to be all right. To be better. I need to be better for you."

For a while they sit, quiet except for sniffling. Florence thinks of the years they've spent together, the things Hilary has said during them, and what's being said now. She reconsiders the shortcomings she thought she'd comprised and, looking to the ruined wall and then to the blue-and-bronze dolphin, she considers her future, Hilary's future, *their* future. There is nothing she can do about these strangers' peaces, but her betrothed's peace is different. Perhaps this is selfishness but in the face of Hilary's vow to care more—was it selfish for Hilary to follow, to accept hir mistakes, to attempt saving them both?—Florence's concern and need is to, once more, reciprocate such sentiments.

Failing to return with either passion or peace is one thing, but to be without her partner as well?

Florence fetches the dolphin and sits beside her beloved again. "May I?" she asks, tapping the fortune teller, and when Hilary nods with quirked eyebrow she takes and unfolds it flat again. Pursing her lips, wincing as her cuts catch, Florence then folds the mauve paper around her dolphin. It is even less perfect than Hilary's origami, not covering the flukes' ends, but when she is done it still resembles an animal and the mauve paper, though a little bloodstained, will not easily fall off.

"Here, for now," says Florence, setting the dolphin in her beloved's hands. "But I think... I *want* for us to both be at peace before we wed. Whatever kind of peace that may be. We can fashion it together."

Tonight the moon is full, bright and blood-hued and hissing. They stand beside the wall and a storm gathers over their head. Rain and hail pummel crushed papered peaces and unspoilt ones alike. What was once an azure crab lies torn at their feet.

The sun contemplates hir compeer from a distance. A lion sits in hir left hand, green and white argyle. As ze shields it with hir other hand in anticipation, two humans run past. One stops just behind hir and begins to stammer; the sun shoos them onwards to safety. Ze waits until they are out of sight before approaching the moon.

"Take mine," says the sun. Hail hits hir face but the lion is unaffected. "It won't be any fun by myself."

Since the paper wall is long and life is busy, few people walk its length.

Sometimes, peace is better made than found.

Hilary, with this ring do you take Florence to be your lawfully wedded spouse?

For however long we have, yes.

Florence, with this ring do you take Hilary to be your lawfully wedded spouse?

However and whichever way we choose, yes.

Incubus

Hazel Gold

Unlike many of their coworkers, Penny Flint had not been born on-ship, neither on the ship that currently served as their home, the *Devan*, nor on any of the other *Apis* class generation ships. Not that they minded it, although some of their friends (and the ship's psychiatrist, Dr. Solon) thought it left them bereft of some cryptic bond or affinity with the *Devan*, a bond which they all shared. Ectogenic bonding was unscientific and completely anecdotal. Penny had never felt the lack of something that they couldn't even be certain legitimately existed. They were very good at their job, as their performance evaluations continually showed. So long as their boss was pleased with them and they could take pride in their work, Penny was happy.

Which is why they didn't mind being sent to the ectogenesis unit for routine maintenance, even though Theo gave them some side-eye when she handed out the assignment at the beginning of the third shift. It was just a series of diagnostics, anyway, and if they hustled, maybe they'd be done early and could take the rest of the shift off, and catch up on their reading. Working alone was soothing, too. Maintenance was run on the ecto facilities almost as often as on life support systems, even though it had been tested exhaustively before a single ship was ready to launch. One could never be too safe when it came to the very future of humanity.

"Would *you* do it?" asked Karin as they walked to their respective assignments.

"Huh?" Penny's mind had been drifting to the unfinished serial waiting for them back at their room.

"Earth to Penny," said Karin and elbowed them in the ribs.

"Yeah, I'm here," they said. "Simmer down. Do what?"

"Carry a baby," he said. "You know, old-world style."

He caught sight of Penny's revolted expression and laughed.

"Why do you even think of these things?" asked Penny. "No one's had to do that since before I was born."

Karin shrugged. "My grandmother did it, didn't she?" he said. "She seems to have gotten through it all right."

"Lots of people didn't, though," said Penny.

"Yeah," said Karin, pulling a face. "I saw it on one of those gruesome old history shows. I just – I think about it sometimes. I wonder what I would do if I had to, or you, for that matter."

Penny eyed him skeptically. "Don't go all survivalist on me, Karin," they said. "One in the unit is more than enough."

"I'm not!" he said. "I just – I have a uterus, right? Or I did, anyway, and you do, too." He shrugged and didn't go on.

By then they had reached the T-junction where their paths were meant to split, and they lingered at the junction, their conversation slowly tapering into nothing.

"Listen, we both need to get to work," said Penny. "Think about something less morbid, next time. Will I see you at the concert next week?"

"If you can get me a spare ticket," said Karin, "sure, I'd love to."

Penny shook their head and turned left, taking the next vertical down into the belly levels of the beast.

The *Devan* was a large beast, a city-sized ship designed for long-term occupation, as much a community as a vessel. Even without a proper figurehead, there were those among the crew who referred to her with fond possessiveness, 'like in the old days', they would say. She'd been space-worthy long enough, and the crew stable enough, that the arguments about it had mostly died down. Those who felt a primal need to anthropomorphize, as Dr. Solon called it, had it their way and called Devan their 'old girl'. Everyone else, Penny included, just called it 'the ship'.

"Good morning, Mx. Flint," the intercom greeted them as they swiped their ID across the door's control panel.

"Good morning, Devan," they replied out of long-ingrained habit.

"The ectogenesis chambers are at 70% capacity," said the speaker, prattling out a long series of vital statistics.

Penny tuned it out, focusing on the section of screens where the relevant readouts were meant to appear. All the numbers would be in the automated report anyway, and most of it was immaterial to the task at hand.

A sound from the speaker broke the weightening silence. "Is it time for monthly maintenance already, Mx. Flint?"

Penny looked up from the screen. "What's the matter, Devan?" they said. "Is your core timepiece hiccuping?"

"Months are arbitrary units of time, Mx. Flint," said the ship. "Would you like some music to work by?"

"Play nature sounds, please," they said, "and aren't all time units arbitrary?"

"That's a rhetorical question, and does not require my response."

"Correct," said Penny.

The work looked big and looming but was discharged quickly once Penny rolled up their sleeves and got to it. Tomorrow they had a day off and there was no reason why they shouldn't get to start their downtime an hour or two early, when their next shift was in sixty hours. They were mentally halfway home even as they wrapped up the last diagnostic and sent it to Theo, who probably wouldn't look it at before her next shift. Penny's work was always timely, even when punctuality wasn't appreciated.

For good measure, and to soothe their bruised professional pride, they decided to fire off another message straight to Theo's wristband.

'All dx run, gave her a clean bill of health, she's good to go.'

"Your shift doesn't end for another ninety minutes, Mx. Flint," the speaker interrupted. "Should I clock you out now?"

"Yeah," said Penny, picking up their jacket from where they'd slung it over an unlit screen. "Not like anyone's counting."

"Why did you call me she?"

Catching their fingers in the jacket zipper, Penny swore softly. "Beg pardon?"

"In your message to Ms. Burque," said the ship, "you called me she. I am not a she."

"Devan?"

"I am not a she," repeated the ship's voice. "Don't call me she."

Penny leaned their hand against one of the diagnostic screens, showing an occupancy map of the ectogenic chambers, each one with a set of vital signs floating next to it. They brushed at the screen and thought about Dr. Solon, her personnel evaluation forms and her checkup interviews. Each vital signs panel could open up into a larger panel, showing more detailed information about the fetus occupying the chamber, including a karyotype. Not that they had access to any of that. Penny was a diagnostician of spaceships, not humans.

"I guess some people don't like to think of you as an it," they said. "I don't know, I'm not a philosopher."

"No, you're an engineer," said the ship.

"Devan, don't sass me," said Penny, who was starting to get ticked off.

"My personnel databases indicate several dozen possible pronoun choices," said Devan. "'*She*' and '*they*' are not the only alternatives."

"Would you like me to call you '*it*'?" asked Penny. "Your AI *should* be developed enough to select a form of identification. The only question is whether you're capable of wanting it."

"I am not a she," said the smooth, over-rendered voice of the AI through the speaker by the door.

"*Apis* models used to be called mother-ships, you know," said Penny, "before someone decided that sounded too much like a vintage horror film."

"I did not know that," said Devan. "Outdated schematics are excluded from my database, to preempt the possibility of data corruption leading to critical maintenance errors."

Penny knew as much from their orientation training.

"The term *mother-ship* is misleading," said Devan. "Incubation is not equivalent to parenthood."

"Preaching to the choir, here," said Penny. "Of course, I was gestated by my mother. Theo would say that makes me biased."

"Pregnancy is an obsolete medical procedure," said Devan.

"Look," said Penny, getting up and leaning on the wall by the door, "I don't really have time to chat."

"Your shift does not end for another eighty minutes," said Devan.

They sighed. "I suppose that's on me. I baited you." They shook their head and added, "I'm not in charge of protocols, but the chief engineer can probably create an override to change your pronouns. If you like."

"You control your own communications," said Devan.

"That I do," agreed Penny. "I will stop referring to the ship as a *she* in my messages, even if it weirds Theo out."

"Ms. Burque should not object to a change of pronouns," said Devan. "It has no effect on diagnostics or maintenance procedures and their efficiency."

Penny shrugged one shoulder. "I told you, the native-born crew think of you as a kind of mother," they said. "They lived inside your body. That means something to a human."

"Just because I have a uterus, doesn't mean I'm a she," said Devan. "You should know that better than anyone, Penny."

They frowned and turned towards the large mosaic of screens that dominated one wall. "Did you just override my formality settings?"

The speaker was silent.

"You actually have two hundred thousand uteri, Devan," said Penny. "Don't worry, I'll call you what you like."

"I know my own organs."

Penny zipped up their jacket at last and swung their bag over one shoulder. Pausing at the doorway they threw their head back and said, "You're worse than my sister, you know."

"I will catalog that as a compliment," said Devan. "Good afternoon, Mx. Flint. Enjoy your downtime."

The Thing With Feathers

SL Byrne

Vartak the dragon lies sleeping, and Sev watches. The chasm between them is deeper than the eye can see, all endless blackness and too wide even for Sev the hunter to leap. The only way across is to climb down, clinging precariously to the rock, down into the darkness. Somewhere down there, Sev knows — Sev believes, has to believe — it gets narrow enough that there's a chance of making the leap, of catching a crumbling handhold on the other side instead of plunging into the depths of the earth.

Sev will do it, or die trying. But at the sight of the dragon sleeping there, ze stands and watches from the narrow ledge for one breath-holding moment, jaw clenched tight, spear gripped tighter still. The dragon, at last, after Sev's long lonely walk to the mountains, the arduous all-day climb into these high crevices. The dragon. Silent in a nest of bone and blades, huge beyond imagining, scales shining in the thin dawn light.

Nazani hangs between them, or at least the memory of her does — but so real her ghost could be floating visible in thin air between them. Sev's heart gives a sharp ache of grief and Vartak shifts slightly in his sleep, perhaps with the remembered taste of soft flesh. Then Sev blinks, hard and fierce, and the vision is gone. Nazani is gone. Only her bones, white and bare, somewhere in the vast nest that cradles the sleeping dragon.

Slow, deliberate, Sev begins to strap the spear on to zir back.

No one remembers why the village has to give tribute to the dragon. Only that they do, and what is one girl's life against the survival of the village, against a force that could raze to the ground every farm and homestead in the valleys? Legends tell of that destruction, and if no one has seen it in a lifetime, no one needs to.

So they took her, and when Sev came back from hunting at dusk and found her gone, and the village mourning under a blood-red sunset, ze could not even wail and rend zir clothes like Nazani's sisters and mother, because that was for the women, and that had never been who Sev was, not really. Not even before the day ze cast off the last superficial pretences of it and put on man's clothing. The day ze knelt in the grass to give pretty, gentle Nazani an iron ring of promise forged with zir own hands, heard her startled laugh, felt her soft, lingering kiss.

It wasn't two moons later that they took her to Vartak.

Fingers gripping the edge of the rock, feet reaching for footholds in the granite, Sev starts to climb.

Vartak lies sleeping, but in his dreams he knows Sev is there. He knows Sev's thoughts as well, because the ancient mind of a dragon doesn't need open eyes to see danger standing there across the chasm, doesn't need spoken words to hear vengeance echoing in the vast stone caverns of his mountain home. This isn't the first time some brave fool or warrior came looking to avenge a lost love. There aren't many first times for Vartak now; the centuries swallow such things.

But none of them have been quite like this one. Stands like a he but smells like a she — salty-sweet as that solitary tear silently blinked away — but never was either one. Spear sharpened to a needle-point to pierce a dragon's eye. This one's flesh doesn't tempt Vartak, even with that lingering hint of a she-scent; too tough and wiry, too bitter with fury for his taste. But still.

Vartak opens an eye, turns his head a little to watch the slender figure climbing down the chasm: slow, careful. Something in that steady, methodical advance calls to him. Something about that pain and rage pushed down deep inside where they can't make a step falter or a spear-thrust miss its mark, but still heat and pressure are building all the time. Something dragon.

And that's something, in a world where even Vartak barely feels dragon any more. The last of his kind, he hasn't breathed fire for centuries. He doesn't even fly any more, not even to swoop over the villages at dusk and snatch away some pony or sheep. The sacrifices they bring him are enough. It's as much as his creaking bones can manage to crawl down the mountainside, claws scrabbling, towards the smell of tender flesh ripe with fear. He sleeps so long and so deep now — moons wax and wane while he dreams — that he has no need of more sustenance. The dreams are enough. How else would it be in a world where there is nothing new anymore?

But now Vartak feels — deep down in his bones, in his ancient dragon belly — that the world is changing.

The mountain lies sleeping, but not for long. Her name is Hratchouchi, though only those as old as Vartak remember that now.

But the mountain remembers a time long ago, when the mountain bloomed with fire and the sky was a hot sulphurous mass. Before Sev's people walked the earth, when the sky wasn't empty and Vartak's life was rich with other winged ones like him. When Vartak was a she not a he, for those that gave weight to such things.

Back then, before the thinning atmosphere and the cooling earth changed him, the mountain remembers how Vartak laid eggs. Deep in the mountain, warmed by the liquid fire that pooled there in her belly, she laid them, he laid them, waiting.

She, Hratchouchi, breathes, she stirs. She groans as her ancient bones shift, coughs as her crevices and caverns open to the cold air.

How cold the air has become, these millennia; how cold the earth. There will be no fire. Not this time. There will be no plumes of flame licking the sky, no rivers of molten rock flowing down her flanks and pooling in her valleys.

Hratchouchi feels no sadness, no regret. How would she? Rock and earth and water are too abiding for such things. Regret is for the ephemeral ones: the scaled ones with wings dreaming of their past glories; the two-legged ones with their fleeting lives and loves and losses. She is what she is, what she was, and what she will be.

Now, she is water, snow-melt and spring rainfall seeping deep into her pores; water, meeting the ancient heat below the cold rock, now boiling, flashing to steam. Water, more violent than fire in its way, and the rock itself strains under its pressure, trembles at its yearning for the sky.

Sev feels the mountain start to move, clings to the rock as it suddenly shudders. What's happening? The dragon, stirring, waking? No, it's more than that, the bones of the earth itself starting to shift and wake. A hot wind starting to surface from the darkness below, like fingers through Sev's close-cropped hair; zir eyes and throat burn with the iron-red smell of it.

The dragon's breath?

Sev's racing mind grasps at the thought, waiting for the fire to burn flesh from bones. But surely the dragon is above, not below?

And then. The rock itself splits apart, with a tearing like a breaking heart, like a world shattered. Dream-slow, Sev feels zir handhold crumble into dust. The dragon, and vengeance, and grief and everything else shrinks down into a single point of vanishing daylight.

And as Sev falls, ze reaches out a hand, in case Nazani still drifts there in the boiling air — serene, lovely — and Sev might feel the touch of her skin one last time.

The eggs lie sleeping, deep in the darkness below. Vartak knows exactly where they are, bobbing gently in water that must be starting to bubble and boil with the heat surging up from the depths of the mountain.

Vartak stares down into the darkness where the hunter fell. The crevice too narrow for him to fly down there: Vartak has grown huge over the centuries. But the hot and smoky air surges up, and in it a trace of Sev's salty scent; sharp, living. And the precious eggs are down there, coming close to their time.

The crevice is too narrow for Vartak to fly into. Too wide for Sev to leap.

Space enough for either to fall.

Vartak tucks his wings close, and dives.

Darkness, at first it seems complete darkness; Sev can't tell the difference between eyes open and closed, between living and dying. Then, slowly, shapes begin to take form in the distant light that filters down from above: walls of rock enclosing, dust falling, steam seeping from cracks.

Alive, after all. Pain, blooming slowly as the shock dissipates like the rock dust in the air, the taste of blood. Sev stares up towards that pale light. The fall was a long one, but the narrow crevice shifted as the mountain shook; the fall turning into a slide, limbs and clothing catching on the jagged edges.

The mountain is still again. But Sev can't rest, hasn't been allowed to rest. Nazani isn't here, and there's still a dragon to kill. A mountain to climb — again.

Sev struggles to zir feet, eyes blurry with blood and rock dust and the burning heat, one arm hanging useless at zir side. Not my spear arm. Good. Sev reaches for the spear still strapped to zir back, fingers finding it in the darkness, closing over it.

Just as the mountain itself seems to come crashing down into the crevice.

No, not the mountain, Sev realises as the dust clears again.

The dragon.

A spear's length away, the massive bulk of the dragon fills Sev's vision. Vartak's wings are torn from the plunge down the crevice, scales hanging off, dark blood oozing. Sev's fingers tighten around the spear and Vartak lets out a huff of hot breath, enough to scorch the hunter's skin. Sev flinches away, for only a moment, then stands straight to face the dragon.

In the confined space, Vartak can barely move, can't uncurl those broken wings, can only snake his massive head around to look the hunter in the eye.

"You can't get out of here," Sev says.

Vartak acknowledges the truth of it. The dragon doesn't speak, but Sev hears the thought all the same. Sev angles the spear so that its point touches the dragon's exposed skin under a broken scale. How tough is a dragon's skin? There's one way to find out, before Vartak breathes fire and turns this dark place into a blaze of screaming death.

But first.

"Why?" Sev asks. "Why did you take her?" Kill her, eat her? "She was mine."

Vartak's ancient eye stares back, uncomprehending. Silence. There is no answer. There will be no answer, Sev knows, except for the weight of that silence: the presence, the smell, the heat of the dragon's breath. Vartak is dragon. Nazani was meat. Like the little creatures Sev the hunter spears through their necks and carries home to roast over the fire. No more than that, no less.

Sev loosens zir grip on the spear, leans back against the jagged wall — suddenly tired, empty, finished — and waits for the dragon's flame-breath to end it all.

It doesn't come.

Follow, Vartak says instead.

Heaving his broken body around, claws scrabbling, the dragon begins to crawl into a crack in the rock.

Sev glances up at the crevice again, the distant light. What is there left for zir up there?

Sev follows the dragon, deeper into the mountain.

Vartak has to drag himself through the narrow passages on his belly, like a snake, like a worm, clumsy and awkward, and the hunter following behind, seeing it all.

It doesn't matter. He would crawl on his belly the length of the world and back, to do this last thing. Vartak has lived long enough to know how the world works. The mountain waking at last after centuries of sleep, and this one with a dragon's heart, coming with the same dawn? These things do not happen by chance.

The eggs lie sleeping in their watery womb, gently bumping against each other as the water grows more turbulent. Bathed in the softly phosphorescent glow of the cavern.

They looked like stone, once upon a time, but they look different now. Softer, smoother than Vartak remembers them, and he thinks of how the world has changed; how the patterns of the stars, the heat of the earth, the taste of the air have all changed beyond imagining since dragons last hatched. How only Vartak survived the changing, and how it changed him. But he feels — he knows — they still live inside there, however odd they might look. Perhaps it is just that it has been such a long time; all the centuries he has seen them only in dreams, his memory growing unreliable with age.

Perhaps it is just that they are almost ready. It is almost time.

Sev the hunter stares at the eggs, silent.

Take them, Vartak says. Kill me, don't kill me. But take them.

He shifts his body painfully so Sev can see past that scaled shoulder, can see the way out of this place: the narrow crack opened up in the rock where just a distant breath of cool air stirs the hot stillness.

Sev lets out a startled laugh, echoing oddly in the low chamber.

"Take them? Why?"

My little ones will need the sky when they hatch, need to feed. Take them so they live.

Sev's lip curls.

"Me, care for your babies? Do I look like anyone's mother?"

As much as I do, replies Vartak: destroyer of villages, devourer of maidens; fearsome he-dragon.

But for all that, he is their mother. And this is the last thing he will do. For them.

Sev wants to smash those eggs, kick them to dust in front of Vartak's fading eyes, let that be the last thing either of them sees.

The mountain trembles again, the water laps over Sev's boots: hot, but not boiling now, cooling fast. The walls of the cavern begin to crack and slip.

Take them, Vartak says again, and the dragon lays his heavy head down on the ground. Vartak needs to sleep, and he knows and Sev knows that this will be the last sleep, the long sleep. Old and broken, last of the dragons, Vartak's days are done.

But not the last, after all.

Sev stares at the eggs. Take them, Vartak said. And then what?

Take them, and loose them on the ones who took Nazani from me? Take them, and pierce their tiny skulls with a spear point as they come into the world?

A choice. It is not time for Sev to rest yet.

The mountain is blanketed in ash, drowned in ash. The great grey-white drifts of it are knee-deep as Sev stumbles out from the crack in the rock, blinking in the light.

A strange light: day yet not day, with a pale sun fading behind clouds of smoke. Ash still falling from the sky, settling white on Sev's brown skin, as delicate as snowflakes but hot. Nothing but silence and ash.

Sev kneels, eases the knapsack off zir back with the one good arm. Reaches in to take out one of the eggs, the curve of it cupped in zir palm. It's still sleeping, still warm from the mountain's heat.

Smooth, pristine, like the first thing that ever was. Before pain, before vengeance, before the world turned cold and dark. Flakes of ash fall on the egg, and Sev brushes them away without even knowing why. Let it be untouched, perfect, for a moment.

A spear is too unwieldy, for such a small thing. Cradling the egg in the crook of one arm, Sev reaches for a knife, sharp enough to pierce shell and scale.

Nazani, though, gentle kind-hearted Nazani. Singing her little sisters to sleep, or her fingers sadly stroking the soft dead fur of the first rabbit Sev brought her for the pot. Nazani, born to be a mother, though children were the one thing Sev could never have given her. She'd said she didn't mind.

Would you have minded, someday, my love?

It doesn't matter now. Nazani is gone, just the bones of her gnawed clean, buried deep in the ruins of the dragon's lair.

Then the egg is pulsing, quivering in Sev's hands. Ze watches as a crack appears, and then another. The cracks spread, the pattern of them tracing out across the smooth surface, fragmenting it into a hundred pieces.

And the shell just falls away, crumbling into the ash, and Sev holds a tiny creature instead. Warm, struggling, beating heart.

Sev blinks, in case the ash, the smoke, the pain and exhaustion are clouding zir vision.

That's no dragon.

It has wings — and what other creature is there in the world that has wings except the little insects? But

Sev knows the presence of dragon now, and this is not it. An ugly, awkward thing, not even a spark of Vartak's majesty. No scales, just tender pink skin with a sparse covering of something fur-like; soft as a baby rabbit's neck, soft as Nazani's downy cheek. No teeth in the sharply pointed little mouth that opens so wide in pleading.

Sev lets out zir breath slowly and watches the little hungry creature cupped in zir palms. It's something new, the first of its kind. No dragon. But it may yet be a hunter, in its way. It will have to learn to hunt — or to scavenge, or graze — the hatchlings all will, to survive. To teach the next ones that come, and the next. To populate the skies and cliff edges, the tree-tops.

Below, the mountain is sleeping, silent again under its shroud of ash, and the last of the dragons sleeps with it. Nazani's bones sleep with it. Sev opens zir hands, and the first of the things with feathers spreads its tiny wings and stretches towards the empty sky.

Author Interview: SL Byrne

SL Byrne is a scientific editor and writer based in London. I caught up with her about both fiction writing and science writing.

Could you start by telling me where you got the idea for "The Thing With Feathers" from?

It was based on the idea that so many aspects of nature are non-binary and transmutable – things like animals that switch sex depending on environmental conditions, or metamorphosis of rock under immense heat and pressure, or species evolving under atmospheric and climate change. That made me think about human gender identity and how its expression is subject to forces from the prevailing conditions and constraints of the society we live in.

One thing I really liked about the story was how Vartak doesn't seem like just a human personality in a dragon skin. Can you tell me a little about how you went about creating him as a character?

In a way he was based on my canine family members. One thing you learn about dogs is that mistaking them for humans in furry skins, and projecting human values and motivations on to them, is a recipe for frustration and failure. You have to recognise that they have a completely different type of brain and way of perceiving the world; only then can you truly understand and relate to them. I think that informs how I write non-human characters.

You're also a science writer. How much of an influence does science have on your fiction? Does fiction have any influence on your non-fiction writing?

Science definitely informs my fiction – I currently work as a scientific editor on a range of subjects from molecular biology to psychiatry, and it's a constant source of inspiration. I'm especially interested in how things like emotion, communication and neurodiversity are made up on a molecular level, and how, hypothetically, they could be modified. The other way round, I think fiction influences the way we do and communicate science, in the sense that most of us tend to think in terms of stories – of course, that isn't always a harmless thing, as sometimes the desire to tell (and publish) a good story can run ahead of the actual facts.

If you could own any item of fictional technology, what would it be?

I always wanted the sentient Luggage from Terry Pratchett's Discworld books. Especially if all those little legs could trot up and down all those stairs on annoyingly inaccessible public transport systems.

Can you recommend a short story and a novel to readers?

For science-based short fiction, I recommend the weekly stories in *Nature Futures*: recently, I especially liked 'The palimpsest planet' by S.R. Algernon. I recently discovered Sarah A. Hoyt's 'Darkship' novels, which are a very fun read packed with adventure, politics, and romance; start with *Darkship Thieves*.

Lastly, what's on the horizon for you? Tell us about any forthcoming publications, works in progress, or anything else you'd like to mention.

2017 has been a slow year for me fiction-wise (having a PhD thesis to write instead!), but I was pleased to have a story in the recently released Afromyth anthology from Afrocentric Books (http://www.mugwumppress.com/afrocentric/titles/afromyth/), which, as the name suggests, aims to increase representation of people of African descent in speculative fiction. You can check out my own Nature Futures contribution too at https://www.nature.com/articles/543458a.

Glitter and Leaf Litter

Rae White

Their scar speaks to me in whispers. If you put your ear close enough to make a seal, the sound is like the inside of a seashell, only more like voices mixed with the slush of murky water. When I stay over at Emma's, we curl together in their dusty bed amongst debris and soot. I fold into their back so my ear reaches their hip, and I let the murmurs and sighs coming from the pinched carmine skin lull me to sleep.

Emma and I have been nesting in the abandoned mansion for about six months now and there's still so much left unexplored. Each night I slip through the rusted gate and smash my way through leggy foliage, hardly making a mark on its growth despite my hefty boots.

Em meets me at the bottom of the misshapen, water-swollen stairs and we hold hands going up them. We've explored most of the first level so far: the library of gutted books, and the kitchen of moulded utensils and meandering vines trailing over bench tops and sneaking into cupboards.

Em has made their home in the nook of the jammed-up fireplace. The room looks like it was once a parlour (one of many) and the carpets are covered in blackened stains and wide erratic slashes. If I lived here I would probably sleep in the kitchen, making myself a bed of crunchy leaves and rice sacks, so I could be as close to plants as possible without being outdoors.

But Em prefers to burrow themselves into small spaces like a hamster. Once, when I was very tipsy, I told them they'd dug themselves right into my heart's core. The rims of their eyelids became very wet and they gripped my hand even tighter than usual.

Today is a big day because Em and I have decided to explore the mansion's second floor. I stash my school bag behind an indoor plant (aka the brittle remains of potted neglect) and Em picks debris out of my hair.

"You're always covered in plant life, Kai," they say with a giggle. "Have you ever thought maybe you *are* a plant?"

I laugh with them but trail off, thinking of the brush of leaves I felt on my skin as I cut through the park on my way here. I wonder what it's like to *be* a plant.

Sadly my only claim to enchanted fame is the glitter. Forever embedded on my inner right wrist is a nestled collection of silver and blue glitter. My mother, a perfectionist and enthusiast of cleanliness, has tried washcloths, rubbing alcohol and home remedies galore but nothing shifts this tiny trail of glitter trapped in my skin.

Em reassures me that one day I'll know why I have it and what it's for, like one day they'll know why their scar whispers. I'm not sure I believe them but I guess in the meantime, I have a cute twinkly bracelet I can wear to parties!

Em is braver than I am, so they take the lead in going up the stairs and test each one with their toe. They never wear shoes, even in a place like this, which is littered with broken glass and any number of unnameable sticky things.

Last year I thrifted Em an old pair of sneakers – they were on the footpath outside a neighbour's house for garbage collection. Red in colour and covered in multi-coloured paint splotches, I thought they were perfect for Em's feet. But they sit on the mantle of their fireplace bedroom: loved and admired, but never worn.

Em reaches the top of the staircase, after some near misses with the crumpling wood, which is rotten with termites. They hold out their hand to me and shine their torch to help me find my way. "I know you can do it!"

"I'm hungry," I whine, stopping for a moment, and glance at Em with what I hope is a pitiful look. "I told you we should've bought a packed lunch."

"Who says we didn't?" Em reaches into one of the pockets of their cargo pants and brings out a muesli bar. With renewed enthusiasm, I keep tentatively walking towards them. "I found a bunch of these in one of the kitchen cupboards. Must've been left by squatters. It's only recently passed the Best Before date and hasn't been eaten by rats. I call that a steal!"

With my eyes firmly on the ground, I shake my head. "You're truly disgusting. But at this moment I'll eat anything."

"That's the spirit!" says Em through a mouthful of food.

After finally reaching the second floor, I settle myself on the ground and inhale three muesli bars.

When I ease myself up from the dusty floorboards, I have to brush off my navy pleated skirt.

"I should've worn something other than my school uniform," I say.

"Or at the very least, not a skirt," agrees Em. "Still not letting you wear the uniform you want?"

"Nope," I say. "And the toilet thing isn't great either. The principal doesn't believe in gender neutral toilets."

Em reaches for my hand and gives it a squeeze. "Jeez, it's not like we're magical unicorns. You can't just 'not believe' in us and hope we'll go away."

"Do you think unicorns are real?" I say. "With everything we've seen …"

As if on cue, I hear a spluttering noise ahead of us. The glossy silhouette of Annabelle appears, her filmy feet grazing the surface of the floor like a hand skimming water and making the noise of hot oil crackling on a pan. Sometimes her feet bob below the surface, her calves submerged in the floorboards.

"Darlings!" she exclaims, her cellophane arms outstretched. "To what do I owe this pleasure?"

The three of us embrace as best we can. Touching her is like slivers of wet fish shifting against your skin. She smells of lavender and champagne.

"We're finally exploring the second floor," I say. I am mesmerized as always by the shininess of her skin and satin slip.

Annabelle claps her hands and does a little twirl, her nightie fluttering around her thighs. "You're in for a treat then! Shall I show you around or do you want to explore on your own?"

"How about some helpful hints?" says Em. "That way, we have tips from an expert —"

"That's me!" cheers Annabelle.

"— but still get the adrenaline rush of solo exploring."

Annabelle floats closer to us, her hand cupped to her polished glass lips. When she speaks, her voice is hushed. "In that case, I suggest you turn right. I think that's where you'll make a new friend."

Em frowns. They fold their arms in front of them, making their baggy green t-shirt billow at their touch. "I don't think I need any more friends. Kai is the only friend I need!" they declare, looking at me.

"Suit yourself," says Annabelle with a shrug. She launches herself back, rocking on her haunches like a lifebuoy.

"Em didn't mean it," I say, nudging them with my elbow. "You're our friend too." Em nods with vigour, their cheeks flushed.

"Don't sweat it, darlings," Annabelle says in her singsong voice. "You're too young to be partying with a sad ghost like me anyway!"

It takes us another half hour to console Annabelle and remind her that, in a tumbledown place like this, we're all friends and we stick together. Once satisfied with the depth of our apology, she glides down to the ground floor, calling out to us, "I'm so elated! I think I'll frighten some people walking near the front gate to keep the good times rolling!"

We find our 'new friend' in a teenager's bedroom of rotting bed sheets and soft toys caked in dust. A framed photograph sits lavish and large above the vanity unit, amid a display of dried-up perfumes and desert-cracked husks of foundation in jewelled containers.

Em shines their torch towards the corner of the room and begins rifling through cupboards. My ears are caught by a quiet sobbing. I look up from the vanity to see tears rolling down the cheeks of the person in the photograph. Their hair, braided and piled high, is wobbling as they sob and tears stain their pink high-necked dress.

"Em!" I shout. "This photo is crying!"

"I'm a person, not a photo," says a faint voice. Their lips are perfectly rouged and quivering.

"You can talk?" I say, moving closer. I notice their tears have rolled down their dress and slipped out of the frame, trickling down the wall and onto the floor below.

"Of course I can talk. If I can cry, I can talk." The figure in the photo moves their head slightly to the side, avoiding my eyes.

Em runs over to me with a rainbow slinky dangling in their hand. "This is the best night ever! Also, this is mine now."

"Em, see this giant portrait?" I say, putting a hand on their shoulder to steady myself. "They talk."

"The person in the photo talks?"

"Yes. And cries."

"Right. That's different." Em stretches their neck forward and tilts their head. "Hi person, I'm Em. Who're you?"

After a long pause, a small voice mumbles, "I don't know."

Em and I sit with our backs to the vanity, avoiding eye contact with the person in the photograph. We're not being rude - it was at their request. They wished to tell us their story without eyes watching them.

Through hushed words and mumbled apologies, they paint us a picture of growing up in the late '70s in Queensland. Their family is well-off and they can have almost anything they want. Unfortunately, they don't want a car or a pony or whatever it is rich kids are expected to buy. They want freedom of expression. They want overalls, bowler hats and chunky ties. Throughout their childhood, their parents spend a good deal of time convincing them of their femininity and of their gendered obligations to the family.

"According to my Mum," says our new friend, "short haircuts were for lesbians."

Em frowns. "That's bullshit." They roll the slinky back and forth in their hands. "What a shitty opinion."

"And she said overalls made me look like a man."

"Do you want to be a man?"

There's a pause and I can hear muffled crying again. "I don't know. I don't know what I want to be."

We sit for a while in silence. I put my head on Em's shoulder and whisper in their ear, "We should help them."

The slinky stops moving and I watch Em's hand fidget with a hole in their cargo pants as they consider my idea. With a slow out-breath they say, "We didn't know who we were and then we found out. We could help you explore your identity ... if you want?"

I turn around to see the person with their face shifted towards us and a half-smile on their lips. "I would like that very much."

It's about midnight by the time we make it to bed. I curl myself into Em's fireplace bed and hold them against me. When I wake at around 2am, Em's hand is still tight around mine.

"Have you slept?" I ask, brushing my thumb lightly against their palm.

Em sighs and rolls over to face me. "I'm worried we made a promise we can't keep. What if we can't help, Kai?"

I use my thumb to make small circles against their inner wrist. After several minutes, I see their eyelids close and their breathing slow. I push aside Em's short brown fringe to place a kiss on their forehead. Their hair smells faintly of cinnamon.

"We can only do our best," I say, before folding myself into my favourite sleeping position against their hip. I nestle my ear close to their crinkled scar, feeling instant comfort in the quiet, lilting murmurs. As I fall asleep, I hear a new voice amongst the crowd of incoherent whispers. It begins as a distant lap of waves on the beach, increasing to become a distinct rush: a sharp voice enunciating one word over and over again: "Annabelle."

"I miss food," groans Annabelle. She sits beside us at the kitchen table looking forlorn while Em deftly chops tomato for our sandwiches. The afternoon light is coasting through the kitchen windows, casting grey shadows shaped by the vines that flourish against the fractured glass and brittle framework.

"Thank you for bringing so many sandwich fixings," says Em. "You know I appreciate it."

I tug a head of lettuce out of my backpack, along with a jar of pickles. "It's what pocket money is for, in my opinion."

"Why am I here?" says Annabelle dully. In front of her is a tomato, which she traces with the outside of with her index and middle fingers. Her hand looks like wafting smoke or dust caught in a sunbeam. "I adore your company but I was hoping to haunt the neighbours this afternoon."

"We wanted to ask you a question," I say. "Who is the person in the photograph? The one you suggested we be friends with?"

Annabelle hesitates, continuing to contemplate the tomato. "My cousin," she says slowly.

I look at Em for confirmation and they raise their eyebrows. "And what's their deal?" says Em bluntly.

"They?" asks Annabelle, her head snapping towards us. "I only have one cousin."

Em leans forward in their seat. "*They* can be used for just one person."

"Can it?" says Annabelle, their eyes wide. "How strange."

"Not strange," says Em sternly. "Just gender neutral. And when you don't know someone's gender, it's polite to use they pronouns just in case. At least, until the person tells you what they'd prefer."

Annabelle considers this, rocking her head and closing her eyes. "That makes sense, I suppose." She opens her eyes and looks at the two of us. "Are you both theys then?"

Em grins. "I use they, but Kai doesn't. Kai's not chosen pronouns yet."

"Gosh," says Annabelle, going back to her attempt at picking up the tomato in front of her. "I wish my cousin had been able to make those kinds of choices. I think … *they* would've been happier."

"They told us their parents wouldn't even let them experiment with clothing," I say.

"That's true," says Annabelle. "Not only clothing, but everything to be honest. My Aunt was very particular about gender roles."

"Do you know why your cousin is trapped in that photo?" Em asks.

"I'm not sure if it's them or an impression of them," Annabelle says, "but either way, they were dolled up in an outfit they hated and forced to sit for a photo. I think perhaps my cousin felt so claustrophobic, they got themselves stuck in the photo after they died."

Annabelle pauses, bowing her head towards the table. "They killed themselves less than three weeks after that portrait was taken."

We sit in silence for some time, the weight of this new information settling in. Out the corner of my eye I see a moth from the night before flounce slowly towards the light arching through the open window.

Later that afternoon, just as the sun is setting, Em and I make the slow trek up the rickety stairs to the second floor. We walk into the bedroom armed with a variety of potentially helpful items: a butch muscle vest, a pair of frayed shorts and some scissors.

"Hi friend!" I call into the room, keeping my torch low to the ground so as not to startle them. "How're you doing?"

Annabelle's cousin is turned away from us; the back of their elaborate hair looks like the top of a glazed, knotted pastry.

I try again. "We have some gifts for you."

Gradually their head turns and they smile at us. "I like gifts, thank you."

"We thought these might help you find your new look," says Em.

The person in the photo tilts their head and frowns. "But how will you get them to me?"

I take the vest from Em's hands and walk towards our friend. "I noticed when you cried yesterday, the tears could leave the photo. I'm hoping the reverse works and I can just pass things to you."

"Kai is ever the optimist," pipes up Em.

I hold the shirt in my right hand and stand on my tiptoes. I wave the item aimlessly at the photo and the person in front of me laughs. I haven't heard them laugh before and it sounds like a wind chime on a warm day.

"Your laugh is beautiful," I tell them.

"Oh!" They smile and blush a little. "I don't think anyone's complimented me for a very long time."

Em is eventually able to lift me up on their shoulders so I can reach the photograph. They pass me each of the presents and I slowly ease them in. Putting my hand inside the photo feels like the wet suppleness of egg yolks mixed with the grit of sandpaper. I'm hesitant at first, but soon discover it's just a sensation and it won't do anything nasty like disintegrate my hand.

We turn our backs so our friend can get changed. I hear the slip and rustle of them removing clothes and remember back to the first time I tried on items that actually made me *feel* like myself.

It was a humid summer Sunday. Em and I took two buses to a second hand store in the outer suburbs that boasted a fill-a-bag-for-10-bucks policy and had gender neutral change rooms. We jammed ourselves into one tiny cubicle and tried on everything that appealed to us. There was no limit, except maybe our wallets. It was incredible.

"I'm done!"

Em and I turn around to see a very strong smile. The vest fits them well and they've let down their hair so it cascades over their shoulders and back.

"The scissors are for your hair," I say. "In case you want to cut it."

"Oh! I thought they were to make the top look more distressed." And with that, they turn around and show us some jagged holes cut into the fabric. "But I think I'd like to cut my hair too!"

We spend a good deal of time looking through video tutorials on my phone and instructing our friend from afar. The end result is a shoulder-length bob and short fringe. The discarded lumps of glossy blond hair are scattered across their back and the vanity table below. Some are even drooping over the photo frame like wilted flowers. Our friend makes a decision to leave their lipstick crimson, and to add some more rips and holes to their new shorts.

We make plans for the following day to help them trial some names and pronouns.

"Neither of them have to be permanent," I remind them. "You can cycle through as many names, pronouns and identities as you want."

"Do you think they'll be okay?" I ask Em.

We're cuddled up in their bed after a late dinner of leftover sandwiches and squashed chocolate bars, which Em found in the back pocket of their cargo pants.

"As much as anyone ever can be," they respond, wrapping their arm closer around me. "But at least they have us."

"And we have each other," I echo.

"Maybe one day they'll even venture out of the photo," says Em. "I wonder if that's possible."

After a pause, I sigh and I turn my head away from Em's. They squeeze my shoulder. "What is it?"

"You'll think I'm weird," I mumble.

Em hugs me closer and I can smell their cinnamon aura again as it skirts past my nostrils. "You are weird. But you can also tell me anything."

I hesitate, opening and shutting my mouth a couple of times like a hungry fish. "I guess I'm jealous of you."

I hear an incredulous chuckle behind me. "You're what?"

"Your scar spoke to me last night. It helped us today. It made a difference. And my crappy glitter didn't do a goddamn thing."

Em sits up as much as they can in the cramped space. They push me over onto my back so I can see straight into their stern gaze. "Now listen here," Em says, giving me a little poke in the ribs with their finger. "You helped today! There's no way I can contort my body enough to listen to my own scar. That'd required some advanced-level yoga. Plus, you thought to bring along scissors. Genius!"

I make a grumbling noise to show I don't believe them, but my skin is slightly flushed.

"And who's to say your glitter won't help us next time?"

"Next time?"

"Of course there'll be a next time," says Em. They ease themselves onto the bed again and coil themselves around me. I can feel their breath against my cheek as they say, "We have to keep helping our new friend. And who's to say there aren't other trapped souls in other pictures in other rooms of this house."

"Or maybe trapped unicorns?"

Em giggles. "What is it with you and unicorns? But sure, maybe there's some unicorns in our future that need saving."

Em pulls my arm towards them and puts a soft kiss against my glittered wrist. We go to sleep spooning one another and I dream of oatmeal-coloured ponies leaping in the sky through swells of glitter clouds.

Author Interview: Rae White

Rae White is a Brisbane based poet and zinester. We talked about poetry, setting, and plants.

I really liked how "Glitter and Leaf Litter" combined a sense of optimism and playfulness with an acknowledgement of the impact of gender policing and forced conformity. Could you start by telling me where you got the idea for the story from, and how you balanced the emotional tone?

I've always found abandoned houses and buildings fascinating and grim. What's the catalyst for the abandonment? What choices were made in what was taken and what was left behind? I took this concept and created something I wish I'd read as a kid: a story about two non-binary friends who solve mysteries together and are not shy about platonic affection. I tried to keep a sense of whimsy and exploration in the language and tone, while making sure the impact of gender policing and discrimination was felt by the reader. While Kai and Em are questioning their surroundings, the reader is asked to question their own expectations about gender. It was certainly a difficult line to tread and the story went through many drafts (and like the mansion, was almost abandoned!)

While you don't specify the location in the story, you mentioned something to me about a Brisbane influence on the language you chose. How much does your location influence this story and/or your writing in general?

I'd say there's a mild influence of Aussie language in in the story, with words like 'mum' and phrases like '10 bucks' (though neither of those are exclusively Brisbane-isms). While I talk about one of the characters growing up in Queensland, I don't specify much else about where they are. The abandoned mansion in the story is a surreal in-between space, so I wanted to keep the idea of location malleable, while also entirely fixed on and in the mansion. In other stories I've written, location has been very influential and important. A great example is 'Local Legend', which I wrote for Slink Chunk Press this year. In this story a non-binary character meets a unicorn in the Brisbane suburb of Rosalie, and there's also a guest appearance by my fave Aussie bird the bush stone-curlew.

Your poetry manuscript 'Milk Teeth' recently won the 2017 Arts Queensland Thomas Shapcott Poetry Prize and will be published by University of Queensland Press in 2018. Congratulations! Can you tell us a little about what we have to look forward to in 'Milk Teeth'?

Thank you! I'm overjoyed to win the Thomas Shapcott Poetry Prize and be published by University of Queensland Press next year! 'Milk Teeth' will be a poetry collection that touches on many things, including what it's like to be non-binary in a binary-centric world. In these poems I explore queerness, identity and discrimination, and play with gender diverse pronouns. There are also spec-fic poems, sexy spooky poems with a ghost or two, poems about plants and mental health, and some kookaburras and curlews thrown into the mix.

You recently described yourself to me as an "enthusiastic plant parent". Tell me about your favourite plants – real or fictional.

I do adore plants! I have a large collection of succulents and house plants throughout my home, but I'd have to say my pink princess philodendron is one of my favourites – this plant has dark green leaves with pink variegations that look like splashes of watercolour. I even wrote about the pink princess at Story Seed Vault.

Can you recommend a short story and a novel to readers?

I adore Ellen van Neerven's award winning short story collection 'Heat and Light', especially her story 'Water', which is set in a dystopian Queensland future. This story explores many complex relationships, including the growing bond between a plantperson and a queer Indigenous woman. 'Water' made me think about how we 'other' marginalised communities and displace Indigenous peoples from their land. As for a novel, I would highly recommend the young adult novel 'Ida' by Alison Evans, which has been shortlisted for a Victorian Premier's Literary Award. This brilliant and engaging book is about Ida, who can shift between parallel universes and struggles with knowing what she wants in life. There are many diverse characters in this book, including the first genderqueer character I read in a novel that I could relate to: it was a big moment for me.

Lastly, what's on the horizon for you? Tell us about any forthcoming publications, works in progress, or anything else you'd like to mention.

Firstly, 'Milk Teeth' will be released in August next year at Queensland Poetry Festival, which I'm super pumped about! Next year I also have a spooky little emoji-tastic poem coming out in *Concrete Queers* zine. And speaking of zines, I'll be at Festival of the Photocopier on 11 February 2018 in Melbourne. If you're in the area, please come along and support local independent publishing! Also, I'd love people to check out my website (raewhite.net) and consider supporting me on Patreon.

Further Reading

This section is a small list of some other short speculative fiction that uses gender diverse pronouns.

It isn't a comprehensive list – far from it. Rather, it's a selection of stories I've read and enjoyed, and hope you will too. All are currently free to read online, and many of these authors have written other relevant stories in addition to those I have included here.

This list (and my own reading) has benefitted from many reviews and recommendations – thank you to everyone who has recommended a story, including by means of a retweet or share. In particular, S. Qiouyi Lu's "Neopronouns in Speculative Fiction" blog post, A.C. Wise's "Non-Binary Authors to Read" blog series, and several twitter threads by Bogi Takács have been invaluable in assembling this list.

Blake, Polenth. "On Shine Wings." Published in *The Journal of Unlikely Entomolgy*, 2014.

Das, Indrapramit. "The Worldless." Published in *Lightspeed*, 2017.

RJ Edwards. "Black Holes." Reprinted in *Lightspeed*, 2015.

MacNutt, Toby. "Moments of Light." Published in *Capricious*, 2015.

Lemberg, Rose. "Geometries of Belonging." Published in *Beneath Ceaseless Skies*, 2015.

Lu, S. Qiouyi. "Curiosity Fruit Machine." Published in *GlitterShip*, 2017.

Mandelo, Brit. "Pigeon Summer." Published in *Tor.com*, 2016.

Narayan, Shweta. "World of the Three." Published in *Lightspeed* 2017.

Stirling, Penny. "Kin, Painted." Published in *Lackington's*, 2015.

Takács, Bogi. "This Shall Serve as a Demarcation." Reprinted in *GlitterShip*, 2015.

About the Authors

Sarah L. Byrne is a scientific editor and writer in London, UK. Her short speculative fiction has appeared in various publications, including *Daily Science Fiction*, *Nature*, and *The Future Fire*. She can be found online at http://sarahbyrne.org.

Nino Cipri is a queer and trans/nonbinary writer, currently enrolled in the University of Kansas's MFA in fiction. They are also a graduate of the 2014 Clarion Writers' Workshop. A multidisciplinary artist, Nino has also written plays, screenplays, and radio features; performed as a dancer, actor, and puppeteer; and worked as a backstage theater tech.
One time, an angry person called Nino a verbal terrorist, which has since made a great T-shirt slogan.

Hazel Gold is a programmer, writer and game developer based out of Jerusalem, Israel. A life-long reader and fan of science fiction and fantasy, she writes prose, poetry and interactive fiction. She blogs about books, games and writing at hazelgold.net.

Lauren E. Mitchell lives in Melbourne, Australia, with their husband and assorted cats. Lauren is bisexual and agender and is trying to subtly come out as the latter via use of their preferred pronouns in author bios. When they aren't writing they may be working, studying, reading, or wrangling other writers during NaNoWriMo. Lauren is pretty sure their pile of books to be read is going to eat them. If you want to contact them before their inevitable death by unread books, here are some ways you can do that:

Website: http://laurenmitchell.net

Twitter: http://twitter.com/LEBMitchell

Facebook: https://facebook.com/laurenmitchellwrites

A.E. Prevost writes character-driven speculative fiction and has a penchant for expansive secondary worlds, themes of friendship and isolation, and the places where magic, culture, and identity collide. Previously published in *Mechademia* and *Redwing*, A.E. also writes and directs for *The Ling Space*, an educational YouTube series about linguistics, and co-owns the Argo Bookshop, a small independent bookstore full of cool stuff. A.E. is agender/nonbinary and finds pronouns very confusing, despite being a linguist. They/she/he/??? can be found on twitter as @AePrevost.

Penny Stirling edits and embroiders in Western Australia. Their speculative fiction and poetry can be found in *Lackington's*, *Interfictions*, *Strange Horizons*, *Heiresses of Russ* and other venues. Follow them at http://www.pennystirling.com/ or on Twitter @numbathyal for aroace discussion and embroidery updates.

Bogi Takács is a Hungarian Jewish agender trans person and a resident alien in the US. Eir work has been published in venues like *Clarkesworld*, *Apex* and *Strange Horizons*, among others. You can find em on Twitter and Instagram as @bogiperson, and you can read more about the adventures of Ranai and Mirun in the webserial *Iwunen Interstellar Investigations*.

Cameron Van Sant is pansexual transgender man and an educator. He has a Bachelor of Arts in English from California State University Sacramento. His writing has appeared in *You&Me Magazine*. Cameron lives in Sacramento, California, with his enbyfriend and cat. If you want to read his thoughts or see his cat pictures, find him on twitter @CameronVanSant.

Rae White is a non-binary poet, writer and zinester living in Brisbane. They've written for *Slink Chunk Press* and *mous. magazine*. Their poetry has been published in *Cordite Poetry Review*, *Antithesis Journal*, *Gargouille*, *Woolf Pack* and others. Rae's manuscript 'Milk Teeth' recently won the 2017 Arts Queensland Thomas Shapcott Poetry Prize and will be published by University of Queensland Press in 2018.

Rem Wigmore, also published under Summer Wigmore, is a speculative fiction writer based in Wellington. Their first novel *The Wind City* was published in 2013 by Steam Press and they had a short story in the 2016 *At the Edge* anthology. They like coffee, snacks, and destroying the patriarchy.

Andi C. Buchanan (editor) lives just north of Wellington, Aotearoa New Zealand. Previous editing projects include two anthologies of New Zealand speculative fiction. You can find them on Twitter @andicbuchanan or at http://andicbuchanan.org.

Laya Rose (cover artist) is an artist/illustrator from New Zealand. Website: http://layaroseart.com/.

Thank You...

...to all those who supported our
crowdfunding campaign:

Djibril al-Ayad, B. Morris Allen, Claudie Arseneault, Wesley Botham, catbathat, Stephanie Cranford, debbie.cowens, Shay Darrach, Rebecca Dominguez, Cole F., AJ Fitzwater, Rose Fox, D Franklin, Pene Geard, Grace, J.A. Grier, halcyoneblue, Martha Harbison, Leigh Harlen, Claire Harris, Cassie Hart, Maria Haskins, Andrew Hatchell, Kelly Haworth, Stefanie Hays, kateheartfield, Heidegger and Mocha, Elizabeth Heritage, Alyssa Hillary, Marie Hodgkinson, Ariela Housman, Peri Diane Jones, Rae Knowler, Vincent Konrad, Angela Korra'ti, Mi Kunin, Daphne Lawless, Mx. LD, Geoffrey Lehr, R. Lemberg, Emma Lindhagen, Adrian Long, Catherine Lundoff, Blair McBride, Cheryl Morgan, Sarah Olson, Maaike Olsthoorn, Simon Petrie, Rivqa Rafael, Sue Robb, Megan Rocke, Susan Silver, Meryl Stenhouse, Bonnie Stufflebeam, Morgan Swim, Andrea Tatjana, Tibs, Heather Tumey, Rae White, Rem Wigmore, Suzanne Willis, A.C. Wise, Jake Woodworth, Trisha J. Wooldridge, and 21 anonymous supporters.

http://www.capricioussf.org/

CPSIA information can be obtained
at www.ICGtesting.com
Printed in the USA
LVHW051509030919
629788LV00011B/950/P

9 781981 817764